Sugar Cain

(Who Can Take Tomorrow?)

horror Shorties by

Christopher E Ellington

Table Of Contents

Dedicated with the love of a child's heart, to The Acri Creature Feature every Saturday Night, from "The Eagle has landed" to "Hello, my name is Jimmy Carter, and I'm runnin' for president". In a better Time and Place, my friend when I had none, and when I had many, my very best.

God Rest You, Chuck.
Deepest Regards, to Bernie the Skull.

"For so long, I've prayed for this...now, I'm sorry."--the words of Isak
Actual Star Trek ("Patterns of Force")

Moderator: And, again on the right, this time—yes?

Student: Dr. Johnsonia, I'm Yianna, I'm in the Honors Exchange Program, pursuing Lab Science in particular...

Johnsonia: Welcome aboard.

Student: Thank you...I'm addressing that, actually, the anxiousness your theories create...*good* anxious feelings... (audience laughter)

Moderator: There are such things. She clarified.

Johnsonia: Pardon me! (audience laughter)

Student: To move out into what can be made, it's sometimes too exciting. Across the board acceptance of the universe as our canvas...we make our *Tabula Rasa.* This opens up vast potentialities, but way more "If". It's a lot to salivate for, given idea of "no resistance", just walking in or onto, out into...

(Background voice shouts, "*I claim this universe for France!*", audience laughter)

Moderator: Ten points. Save it, though. Please.

Student: Well, before planting *any* flag, before utilizing what we tap, harness...we have to get there. And develop what we know, what we are, what we have and can create, in order to get there.

Johnsonia: We're “there”, now, if a basic cable package works for you. The resources of what we may find in order to go find more, can be realized locally, and the inner universe, without question--it all depends on the 'what', and these days, how deeply disapproved, that 'what'...then, if you begin toward success. As a laboratory scientist, here, are you...what, you're asking about Man?

Student: Primarily. You can't harvest without workers. To do this job of improvement, if it really is out there for taking, raw materials, building blocks of knowledge... The prerequisite would be Man as able to work, effort in full, to be worthy of what the human race is reaching toward.

Johnsonia: Omigod...if this was a private conversation, I'd go on how lovely that belief as stated, is. For lecture hall purposes, you're running with the paradox of the breed. *“How do we weave a cloth with our dirty hands, to clean the stains off our hands?”* I admit to you, that's out of my depth. I can prove the high finite watershed of Everything, will yield to uses of Human. How you get a better human with better use needs, Mary Shelley already failed at and Tokyo hasn't yet learned.

--from a recording of the Q&A period following Dr. Prescott Johnsonia's lecture, “Fearing the Placid Universe”, Emory University, September 28th, 2004

Glue Gun

The smarmy young man scuttled away with his beer. The watermark on his check, Canadian, had scanned on the fifth try; at that, it had taken help at the front desk. Conchita, who'd run into more than her share of junior scammers when working third shift, curled a lip at his retreat. Then she sweetened it friendly, greeting the poor woman who'd had to wait so long.

“Hi. Sorry about all that. We can't take chances on out of town checks.”

“It's all right,” slurred the woman, head bowed to obscure her features. Clearly, it was *not* all right. The matron looked sad and in pain. She'd been in bad shape when she'd first gotten in line, half an hour before. When the punk with the suspect Canuck check gooped up the flow, Conchita thought she'd heard the woman cry a little. She wanted to ask if she could help, but Jollop Market frowned on that. Conchita's best friend had gotten fired for offering an old man an aspirin.

The woman's skin was rumpled, loose, slack. That's what was “wrong”, as otherwise, she was fine. Light, eye-catching tan. Outfit simple, but youthful. Hair, the tricolor of old towhead locks...though, Conchita wanted to laugh, at the styling. Wanting scissors and products, wavy and frizzed, the woman's hair had recently been a feather job worthy of Farrah. Before whatever... The old broad (was she old?) looked as though she'd been shut up in a closet.

The woman was shy. Replies were whispers, short and moist. Mushing, her words. Conchita felt sorry for her, but you had to ask about coupons, and you had to do the "paper or plastic?" number, and nowadays, you had to ask if they had their Jollop Dollop with them, that stupid name the CEO had given the discount card. There were only five items. They should have opened the Express Lane for her.

By the end of the dance, the woman was near-distraught. Conchita smiled at her, trying to be pleasant. It wasn't easy. The woman (20? mid-40's? 82?) had a definite problem, and it was all in her appearance. By now, the cashier had gotten a good gander. The matron was hideous. Worse even than when she'd gotten in line.

The woman's eyes were sunken, so deep it evoked the word "undead". Her shoulders slumped, apelike, cartoonish. Eyelids hung as a stroke victim's. Earlobes, echoing a baby puppy. Cheeks caved in far enough, one would think she was toothless, but when she spoke—if you could call that speech—pearly whites, perfection, better dental than Conchita had enjoyed since junior high. It all made for a human contradiction: the woman was young and old, both vibrant and ancient. Maiden and crone, together. Plain to see, without perceivable sense. Conchita rang her up, conversing as little as possible. Recalling Grandpa Orlando's tales of a man he'd known in Juarez, a cursed man who grew dirtier and filthier no matter how he bathed, until eventually he lived as the earth beneath their feet.

The matron paid in cash. She was red with embarrassment. *I don't blame you*, thought Conchita, counting back change. *If I looked like you, I'd never leave the house.*

"Okay," she said to the woman, who was already hurrying off, trying to hide her face as she went, "Thank you, and have a great day."

The matron acknowledged like someone speaking while pigging out. For a person trying to rush away, she pushed the cart with increasing difficulty, older and softer than a minute before. Conchita, who had left the Roman Church and become pagan the year before, crossed herself.

She was staring as Mike, the store's "third man", stepped behind her.

"I have to print a copy of the receipt for home office," he said. "That foreign check is scanning wonky, again. I bet that little shit used xerography."

The matron was pushing, painfully, through the far exit. Conchita barely felt herself move, or Mike take over the register.

"Michael. Who is that?"

"Hmm?" He was tapping, entering numbers. "Oh! Mrs. Boland. Yeah, she comes in once a month, maybe twice. They used to be regulars, but the husband developed panic disorder and lost his job. They shop at Brice Discount, now, or out at the Wallie World superjiggie."

"No, I don't mean that, I mean...her looks! What's with

that?"

"Oh." Mike grinned over his shoulder, then cleared a mistake and entered the data again. "That's right, you've always been third shift, before. Don't let her fool you. Mrs. Boland is one of those "good days and bad days" people, in spades. Trust me, if she came in tomorrow morning, like as not, she'd look younger than you."

Conchita, 29, made a narrow face.

"Whaaat?"

The register was printing. Mike nodded at it as he answered her.

"Kid you not. Her husband's the luckiest man on the planet. The term 'drop dead gorgeous' is on her driver's license, I think. Mind you, she shows up looking like an extra from *Charlie's Angels*, but there's something to be said for that, too."

They were facing each other as Mike sidled out of her checking niche.

Conchita blinked. "I think you're batsy, Michael. Your Elvis has left the building or something. She looked like an old damned woman--old, young, both, but she could barely stand! She looked ready to melt onto the floor! Melt! Like a popsicle!"

Mike was suddenly Company Man, fixing her official displeasure.

"People aren't popsicles, Conchita. I hear she has a rare muscular disorder. Has to rest a lot. Once heard a rumor about water weight gain. But she's been coming in since I was a bagger. *Customer*, as in 'long term'."

He frowned away from her register. Conchita, stung,

called after him.

"What did I say, I didn't call her no names or nothing! *Michael...*"

She glanced back, at the exit. Conchita felt queasy. Again, she thought about the soil of Juarez.

The ignition was stuck in locked position. This happened more and more. Nichole wept without tears. She'd stayed out too long. It had been a hard, terrible day. First that old jerk of a postmaster, then the dumb blonde at the bank...all the fiddly things on her To Do list. She shouldn't have stopped for the ground chuck and spices, but Troy wanted his Joes, and he did so much for her...

"Start, goddammitt!" she shrieked at the the steering column, voice that of angry wind and rain. Her fingers drooped, soggy noodles, around the ignition. She had to make an effort. Jiggled it. Cajoled. Put into it what strength remained.

She quaked with fear of discovery. She wouldn't make it this time. Everyone would know. They'd throw rocks at the mayor's house, well, good, Rex was an asshole, but her life with Troy would be over. Nichole in a bucket in some lab, Troy flashfrozen before Intelligence, or worse, before media. Anderson, Oprah... Troy would kill himself. She couldn't let that happen.

The ignition unstuck. The little Pontiac roared. Nikki peeled out of the lot.

She cut through old downtown to make it home faster. Through the burned out area, north end of town. The ghetto. Where the skin trade had flourished for a million years, before beloved Mayor Cromwell shut it down. *Uhuh.* Rex gave the police *carte blanche* and closed his eyes. The block war during Y2K had killed 50 people. Why didn't that score national attention for more than seconds? Because it was Rex Cromwell. What happened to the son really happened to the daughter.

The silver Lemans had poor pickup. The man at the garage said it was operating on three cylinders. Nikki had it floored. The car left stoplights at a crawl. Zero to 40 in a minute and a half. Nikki felt her internal organs flattening, the prelude to liquifying. Her skin was becoming clay, and moist. It would be visibly damp in a moment, then wet outright. Sticky bubblegum, and it would hurt when Troy took off her clothes. Her insides were screaming. Nichole was crying aloud. No water from her tear ducts. There never was. You didn't secrete yourself.

Forty-five mph by ten blocks away. Fifty-five, by six. She blew down Fender Street, the haunted place everyone avoided, because it saved a block. Nikki gunned it through a four-way stop. Her foot had less and less pressure on the pedal. The Lemans chugged, old campaigner. Old like her, but not. The Pontiac Lemans had maybe two more years. Nichole Herrick-Boland, was eternal. Gilgamesh H2O.

By rote, foolish, always the good little homemaker, she took her groceries in with her. Nikki slipped, skulking, around the back to the screened porch. A neighbor almost saw her, but was distracted when his cell rang. She made it inside, to the kitchen. She sought Troy, who was plying his talents at the iMac. Said talents earned little. Nikki shuffled to him. Shambled. Slid forward, human slug.

Troy Boland was happy, if only for a moment, lost in his world of imagery. Troy was 47, but younger now than ten years before, if only by how he lived. Troy had worked at a brokerage firm for twenty years after community college. Then, his father died, and for awhile, they'd had money. In the middle of settling Pop's affairs, taking care of Nikki and holding down fifty hours, Troy snapped. A panic attack while down in LA, on Alameda St. during rush. He ended up abandoning their car, an import promptly stolen. He'd run for three miles or more. He flew home. That was in 1999.

He was a hack writer and blogger, doing enough medical transcription they kept the utilities on. Pop Boland's money was long pissed away. Somehow, they kept having a little money, surviving. Troy never spoke about that.

His wrists ached. They snarled at him. He had carpal tunnel, severe, but they'd lost their insurance when he'd been canned. Nichole told him he needed to work, but in-home jobs were limited, and usually preceded by some fee. Troy, after an abortive attempt, now refused to get behind the wheel. Nikki ran errands, took care of him. In his way, as now, he took care of her.

"Troy...!"

"Ni...Oh, God! *My God!*"

"im lade," she...slushed. Nichole's face had melted, two parts crone, four parts George Romero zombie, a dash of Dr. Phibes. Mostly, she was boneless Sharpei. Her lower lip, that of a dynamite pouter, hung a full inch beneath her chin, revealing bell-curved gums. Her bright white teeth were superheated Christmas divinity, curving in kind.

Troy leapt from the chair, grabbing her grocery bag, flinging it aside. Second nature, he quickly undressed her. It was worse if the clothes got caught up in her. Took sometimes a week for scar tissue to work itself away.

Nichole stood, limp, unable to help her panicking, gasping husband. With little difficulty but just in time, her ensemble slid free. The body beneath was teen-young, yet blasted by a wrinkle bazooka. A big, rumpled skin suit. Pajama person. Laundry nudity. Nikki's breasts were down below her waist. Her navel, collapsed shut. Her light glaze of tan, beginning ooze.

Nikki dripped, falling in beach bunny slag away from her skeleton. But there was no skeleton. As though a waxen doll in noonday sun, Nichole Boland imploded in hunks and chunks, washing faster and faster to floor. Troy, having removed her clothes seconds before they would have become harmful, watched. He waited until he was sure they were ready for the next step. He hated it when Nikki did too much. He knew it was his fault.

"yii...buhd...", Nikki said, syrup with a voice. Troy knew this as "I'm bad", but answered it only with the calming shush a parent extended a child in distress. He told Nikki it was all right, told her he loved her. Then, he stepped away.

In the time it took to zap a bag of carmelcorn, Nichole became a large puddle on the floor. Troy was ready, '9ers wastebasket in hand. Galvanized. The super size, right from their website. Absolutely spotless. He braced it between bare feet, pulling rather than whisking with the broom, bristles trapped safely in rubberbanded plastic wrap 4 ply strong. The slop of Nichole went in, easy enough.

Only at the very last did the melt of Troy's lifemate grow sticky. A tiny strip of whitepink glaze hung over the edge of the '9ers basket. Troy shifted fast to knees, and like Duke Wayne on a first take, whipped a toothbrush out on the fly. As opposed to killing the bad man, Troy's job involved wielding the cleaning instrument, expert. Adept at salvage. Six swipes, seven, eight, and the last of the "stick" had gone in. Barely. Clinging near the basket lip, some of it.

Troy peered into the can. Color splotches of soup. *No, honey, you aren't bad. And it isn't a bad day. Just a day.*

The next part was always worst. Troy was not a young man, at least not by his own, unforgiving standards. He pumped iron irregularly, but the strength this required, had become itself a hurdle to clear. He made certain his grip was tight. Properly, he lifted with his legs. The waste can of Nichole blocked his vision, but Troy knew their house blind, a burned-in screensaver. He'd left it exactly five times in the last year. Troy Boland was calm, now. He'd surprised himself, doing shit correctly.

Since the panic disorder, he'd begun to wonder if he was good for anything. Living with said panic, made their lives too complicated. He hadn't driven since the days of William Jefferson Clinton. To even be a passenger, he had to take enough Xanax that, as soon as returning home, he slept the rest of the day. The money situation was Titanic on FF-PLAY x2--although, even monied, Life for the couple had been a conjuror's trick.

Naked and kicking playful in his arms or a honkin' can o' soup, Nikki was always dead weight. Troy grunted, for the first eight stairs. He groaned, the rest of the way. The small bath down the upstairs hall greeted him, goal. Pained wheezes, as he set her down. Troy hunkered. Observed the soup, light tan and salt-white. He had to judge by depth perception, alone; Nikki knew when he'd checked consistency with a finger or instrument...the last time, she'd slapped the back of his head, next morning.

Yes. More watery. It would be thin enough, in another minute, to pour. Troy didn't rest. *Check adjustments, check adjustments.* He made certain the drain of the sunken tub was shut. He then carefully applied a vulcanized rubber mat, thick and strong, atop it, for insulation. He rested, for perhaps five minutes.

Troy wiped his face. His sweat felt cold, the perspiration of the sick. These irregular DefCon emergencies always left him weak and trembly. At that, they got the thing over with better than Nik wanting like some kid to stay up until she couldn't stand it. Troy often got mad at her. *Why torture yourself? Lie down in the tub! It'll be better in the morning!* Nikki knew that, but fought it, most days. She wanted to be with him, she said as defense. They needed as much time together as they could steal.

The money situation was worse than ever. God Bless America and the fruited plain. Troy had sold most of his rare books, all his WW2 paraphernalia. He'd have to call Rex again, soon, and he didn't want to call Rex. Troy knew he'd get whatever he asked, but he didn't like calling...once, he'd sold Mom's emerald ring to put it off another two weeks. Troy didn't want to be near Rex Cromwell. Rex was an asshole, a charming asshole, but there you were. The central orifice of a big, fat fundament. Rex should be dead and in Hell. It was no comfort, knowing what had happened was spirit stuff. Rex, in a world called 1979, had been like them, just another teen with his cherries up for grabs. Nothing about the incident made sense. Troy no longer tried to reason it in the physical.

The bathroom stank. Troy knew it needed scrubbing. Nikki always told him he as such a slob, but he cleaned her up nice, and if it hadn't been for the panic...

1979, hadn't smelled bad. Youth, never did. It often felt bad, tasted foul. Looked dicy. Sounded loud. But, scent? Life's perfume. It smelled like New. Troy closed his eyes, and there it was, again. Mind pictures. Snapshots of unfulfillable longing.

Nichole, sundrenched skin, golden feathers of hair. Body at once hard and soft, perfect fit and pliable flex. Tight Calvins. Blue spaghetti straps. Wearing her flats.

Melting, sky blue orbs, afire. Beach angel face, inhuman. Screaming at Rex Cromwell, to die.

The school patio. The stone tables, the wide area in-between. When they'd torn down Templa High in '98, of course that all had gone with it. The collage of *faux* baubles and cheap cement. The palm tree, there, in the corner. It was to Nikki's left. There were kids to her left, as well. At least three people, were close enough to intervene. No one did. No one helped. Frozen as the neighbors who watched Kitty Genovese killed, or as children brought up on the tube. Frozen, maybe, because Rex was an asshole, and assholes deserved to die.

Everyone knew what had happened. It was all over the school. Rex had been Nikki's consort for many months, until just the week before. He'd always used her and treated her badly. But this last bit...how could anyone...

Dana Elmore was shrieking murder. Lorna Jensen bawled like a child. Herbie Silverman, now the toughest prosector north of LA, sprinting off, *"Gangway!"*, like in some Gilligan episode. A jock, swearing at Nikki. Some burnout, catcalling Rex. Rex, ego size of the Bay Bridge, sarcastic, invincible. Calling her a hooker and a whore. A few other cheap, dirty names. Saying "take your best shot". Turning away, bird in salute.

Boom. Boom.

With care and precision, Troy Boland lifted and tilted. Talked sweetly to Nikki as he poured her into her insulated bed. He knew she kind of understood him, kind of not. Nik said it was like the "dream speech" in *Twin Peaks*. Tone of voice, was most important, she said. *Like you're speaking to a cat.*

They didn't dare keep a pet. As for the other, Troy had gotten a vasectomy at 20, back when they hurt a long time afterward and couldn't be reversed. Even today, with advancements in the speed of tubal ligation, it wouldn't have been feasible. Nichole, with little stress and minor strain, could maintain consistency for a max of fifteen hours. More realistically, twelve. It had been easier, before he'd come down with panic. Troy had worked, tireless, running home three times a shift. Carrying a beeper, "in case". Now, they were hamstrung. It wasn't likely to change. Between both their handicaps, he knew they'd never move.

Nichole, watery, now the darkened clear of dirty rain, flowed into the tub. Troy kept the can tipped, for more than 10 minutes, a necessary precaution. When Nichole was 17, the day she'd fired two bullets through Rex Cromwell, she'd been over 5'6". Today, three decades on, she stood exactly 5'4". When she stood. Relative frame unchanged. What liquid they'd lost in all that time, showed by way of height.

Troy kept watch on the overhead clock. Ten minutes more off their lives. What life you'd call it.

The '9ers can held only now, a bare sheen. Troy dug, anyway, methodical with the toothbrush, until the can was dry. He set it aside, and aching, stood, then drew the shower curtain to cloak her shame. He left, flipping things dark on the backhand, closing door until it latched.

He returned to his computer. It had slept itself. Troy shut it down. He went to their small kitchen, and made himself a sandwich. PB&J. Boring. He wanted to fry up the "Untidy Jose`'s"...but, they were supposed to eat, together. Troy felt big on "unfair", just now. He ran Nikki every day, ran her until, about once a month, this happened. For what?

He made nothing with his online indie endeavors—print expression was too common, so worth little. The medical transcription scored enough—barely, if you liked no cable, thrift store clothes, canned pasta and water... For Christmas last year, they had eschewed presents for one another, agreeing on a Roomba for the house. "I want that floor so clean, I can puddle on it!" Nikki had laughed, too hard. Always, exaggerated effect. Trying to let him know it was okay. That Life didn't suck. Troy wanted to believe that, but it had been easier, at 30. Easier still, at twenty-five. Easier if he hadn't knocked at her parent's door, on just the right day.

He sat on the screened back porch, 8 x 8, a bitty little cell. A mower plowed along, near-distant. The guy in back, was yelling at his dog. Troy realized his cell phone was in his hand. It took more than half an hour to make up his mind, punch in the digits, hit Dial. The mayor's secretary put him straight through.

Toward evening, he stood on the front stoop, waiting. Xanax popped, 4 ½ mg., after two halves already that morning. Troy swayed. He teetered. He knew neighbors thought he was a drunk. Whatever. Better they think that.

Sedan De Ville. Baby puke yellow. Rex's own car. It pulled to curb without honking. A plainclothes detective slipped out the passenger's side and trooped up the walk. The man, always the same guy on these occasions, nodded once, wordlessly accepting the house keys. Letting himself in. Troy was all right with this; every time the professional courtesy had been needed, he'd arrived to find the policeman, armed, seated on a hard kitchen chair, 10 feet inside the door. The guy was probably all right. Troy prayed to God.

Rex greeted him with a single, generic syllable. Troy nodded. He was dressed in his last, good suit, tan corduroy, the only decent thing in the closet...but next to Mr. Hugo Boss, Troy felt like a Bible salesman.

Brief talk on the way there. About the money. Money matters were kept private, something Troy respected.

"How much you need this time?"

Troy hedged.

"How much of the Ordaz money is left?"

Sarcasm, from Rex. Sarcasm, was something he was good at. It was his milieu.

"That's a genius question... You're not getting everything I have. Besides, it's invested. Jaquie'd snap me off, if I started letting investments go. I told you I could go sixty-large per annum in a broad sense, but the more you need, the slower the eggroll. The less you need, the faster I can pay out."

Troy didn't feel like a beggar. He and Nichole had

this coming. Nikki, especially. This was Rex paying dues. What happened to Troy's love, long before he'd slipped the band over her finger, was all on Rex's ledger. Rex, who'd once hit her. Rex, who'd taken nude shots of her and showed them to his friends. Rexford C. "Re-Elect Me, I shut down the Ordaz skin ring!" Crowell, who'd bullshitted Nikki into turning an actual trick. Witnesses, who knew her, placed discreetly, to observe the exchange of cash. A microcassette recorder, in a motel drawer. The john, a guy from another school, whom Nikki was told was an out-of-towner. Telling everyone Nikki humped for Hate Ordaz, the craziest pimp in the world. Somehow getting in no trouble, himself. The thing she'd killed him for.

Troy had the moral high ground. The upper hand, too. Sort of. But Rex sailed his boat free on a sea of selfjustification, and Troy knew Rex thought himself magnanimous for helping at all. Troy could push it balls to the wall. Rex would probably have him killed. A man who patted himself on the back for stacked cords of dead people, be they hookers or officers in the line, held life on the cheap. Rex was sorry for all he'd done to Nikki. Rex was penitent. But only to a certain point.

Rex, again. Matter-of-fact.

"We can just do the stipend, Troy, and stop pretending we're friends, but that means no more the three-point-two a month. I'll set it up direct deposit. Tomorrow morning, if you like. But then, I don't want to hear about a toothache, or a muffler problem, or a red satin dress for her birthday. Okay?"

Troy watched the ocean roll by, to his side. City of water, an empire more vast than any of men. The Caddy slid along a bridge, hugging the cliffs, and the beach smiled up at Troy. Nikki was on the beach, laughing, tossing wet feathers, Steely Dan janging mystical on a radio, nearby. The beach, the sweet cold Pacific, and Nikki. They smelled of New.

Rex was watching him, glancing from the road to Troy and back again.

"You think about it, bud," he said, underscoring the tack. "Let me know."

The nice place, just South, by the ocean. Ruhlin's. Expensive. Troy and Nikki hadn't been, in long years. There was valet parking, but Rex preferred to do it himself. Lots of genteel, quiet, *hello, mayor,* from entrance to table. Rex had them seated privately, in the banquet room.

Patient and polite, until served the main course. To then, conversation consisted of Rex's civic administration, his chilly relationship with his frigid, society wife, his love affair with himself, and why he'd always hated Joe Montana. Same shit, different epoch. Rex Cromwell was an asshole. Probably why he'd gone politics. Why he got things done. Why, if you thought about it, people kept voting for him.

Hot plates of coq au vin and Alaskan king crab were placed and help, nodded away. Rex brandished a fork, ready to begin.

"I've been wondering for years, why you never asked. Every time, it would hit me, on delay: '*Oh. Yeah. They don't like me.*' Nor would anyone else, if the thing came to light--some, would believe it, enough it mattered. I could slip the bonds of accountability, but I've known forever I'd only rise so high. Big fish in a koi pond, yippee-I...but, the instant she hit the trigger, I was too hot a property. I've spoken with political 'agents' over the years, top smooth-over guys, like Carville. We always get to 'Why didn't you die?' or 'What happened to her?', and I dummy up. Hem and haw. This'll be huge, the rest of my life. 'Guess that's *my* sacrifice."

Troy looked up from cracking into a claw. His voice was a bit too loud.

"You're comparing?"

Rex darted eyes to the room entrance. He waited. Relaxed. Shrugged.

"Why not? It's all relative. Then, when I paid out to you the first time, I said, that's the end, Rexford. You played, and you finally paid. I gave up. I'm Mr. Mayor as long as I'll probably want, and I'll make do. What a loss. And with all that's happened. *9/11. Right.* Not on my watch."

As punctuation, Rex threw back a draught of Johnnie Walker.

"So, today," he continued, "It's not so much water...*blood* money, but you want to hear the story. Unexpurgated. Sounds good. I loves me a tale—and I'm the star! Sure, why not?"

With that, Rex tucked in. Troy sat, waiting, as everyone always had and did. How this asshole had pushed to within shouting distance of 50 years old, still believing the universe his hula hoop, was astounding.

Rex savored the chicken, for minutes. Complimented the tender carrots. Sipped his Johnnie Walker, slow. Troy gave up hope. Then,

"You remember Pat Isador? Older kid, lived across the street from me? Good lookin' guy? Turned out he was gay?"

Troy blinked. "Is that the guy they say became a ghost? Over on Fender Street?"

"No, no, *no*...that was Von Wisher, and Von was younger than us. *Pat.* Tall guy? Complexion problem? Head like a hairy pencil eraser?"

Another blink. "Oh! The Marine?"

"Bingo" fork stab.

"Yeah! Pat Isador. Pat was four years my senior, and we hung out all the time. Creative, funny. Any other people around, though, he'd treat me like sewage. Hazard of being the tyke.

"Well, Pat and I, it's a rainy summer day, I'm about 9, we're listening to his mother's 78 shellacs. Spike Jones. Beautiful stuff, priceless kitsch, we turned it into garbage. We're bored. He doesn't want to play soldiers, I don't want to play his baseball stat game... We end up blurting out funny things, lines. We used to do skits all the time for his mom, silly stuff.

"We start trying to make old rhymes into new ones...Mother Goose, Little Golden material. Like that. We degenerate to doing it with simple doggerel. Schoolyard taunts, for example. We get hung up on *I'm rubber, you're glue, everything you say bounces off me and sticks to you.* It's clunky, too many syllables. I have a few go's, can't do anything. I remember saying we should throw out the word "glue", but still make it about "what goes around comes around". Which, is what it is, that taunt, really. Reciprocity.

"It's storming, outside. Rain's coming in barrels. Pat goes all quiet. I open my mouth, but he waves me shut. Then, I hear him, hardly at all, even with a kid's hearing, *I barely even hear him*, voice as strange as I ever heard. He says, just below the big rain,

I'm rubber, you're water,
What happens to the son
Really happens to the daughter.

Rex smiled, adream.

"I loved that tercet. It moved me. I memorized it, right then. Some dumb mantra for me, I dunno. When I threw out my parent's church in 11th Grade, I went through this period for about a month, this weird thing where I'd kneel down before bedtime, like a little boy saying prayers...except, all I said, over and over, was the tercet. My breath prayer. And it wasn't to any god."

Rex mugged, a "*What, me worry?*", and resumed stabbing his coq au vin. Chilled, Troy laid aside knife and fork. There was no god. No mercy. Not to make a creature like Nikki live.

He said, "But what does that have to do with it? You called her names. You didn't recite ditties."

"No, but I was thinking it. At the forefront of my mind. Like when you talk to yourself, in your head, a private tea party with your brain? Internal dialog. I was thinking Pat's rhyme. Screaming it.

"I know I looked cool, Troy. Screw you, bitch, and all like that. Are you kidding? Nik had a Saturday Nite Special, on me! I knew she'd drop the hammer. It was too big not to. I just...*thought* the rhyme in my head, screamed it, in my head...because I thought maybe, somehow, it would protect me."

Troy had left off eating, hands in his lap.

"And it did," he said.

Rex shoveled up a piece of chicken.

"Yeah."

"Tell me how."

Chewing. Sipping. Mistrusting eyes. Dab of napkin. Elbows to table.

"I didn't hear the gunshots. I mean, Troy...maybe, yeah, but they were wrapped up in my scream, the kiddie rhyme. I remember turning away, flipping the bird, and the words took off, a jet streaking the sky. I was propelled, but more like a feeling, even the sound was a feeling! Propulsion. All of me, all I am, blasted into...I'm not religious, Troy, so when I say it was all white, don't think wings and halos, or golf tees with Ben Franklin in the foursome. 'White', is the absence of color. I was shot like a projectile, through the absence of color. Except, I was only the rhyme. Maybe because it came so primal. What Christians call the 'spirit man'."

Rex reached, lumberjack, for more bread. Slathering the real butter upon which he'd insisted. Troy sat, limp, rag doll prop in the Cromwell eternity.

"Then, the white explodes into reality," intoned Rex, when finished with his bread. "First time I ever saw digital cable wink then rebuffer, I threw up, because that's precisely how the world came back to me.

"I'm at the Fabron Isles police station, the old one, natch. A policewoman's grilling Nikki while some old detective plays Mr. Grandad. I can hear the words: *They're gonna tear you up in Chino, babycakes! You're going inside for all day!* Nikki's not scared, though, chin up, like she'd get? That look that says the cop's what she left on her plate, last meal. I don't think of her as having killed me, although by then, I'd have been pronounced. Hell, I'm not angry. I'm not a person. I'm a rhyme! ...and, maybe I'm a bit of truth, as PI as that would be taken, today."

Troy's throat was dry. He looked at his water, looked at his Coke, but made no move.

"So, you're truth," he said. "How'd you make yourself stick?"

Rex grunted at the twist of phrase. He munched his carrots. Continuing the tale as though alone. Really enjoying the company.

He said, "I drift downstairs. They have some of Hate Ordaz' chickies in on battery, not solicitation, oh, no, everyone before me always winked at that! Well, but, one's a Romani, and I could tell, I just knew... It comes to me, in this spirit consciousness: *She'll understand.* I go into her head, to see through her eyes while still being me, the rhyme, my truth. She's cuffed, but only forward, and when she wanders away, they just let her.

That Ordaz cabal always got a free ride; I made them my personal mission, once in office. That's well gone...

"She's up the stairs, slomo. I'm looking out of her like it's the observation deck on Miss Liberty. Some genius thought in a robot-brain. They're dragging—*dragging!*-Nikki out of Interrogation, telling her it's the lock-up, they'll be sure to send her down some friends. Nik's cussing, yelling. Telling them I deserved it, I'm an asshole. Telling what I did, saying it at the top of her lungs. The lady cop tugs one way, Nikki yanks diametric, and Grandpa Good Guy steps in the middle—but, Nik hasn't been recuffed. The grips on her slip off, and both women fall to the floor. The lady cop goes headlong, bangs said head, then gives Gramps an earful, for his efforts. Meanwhile, my Romani host is kneeling beside Nikki.

"Nik freezes up, afraid for the first time all day, only because she doesn't get this. My host places her hands on Nikki's chest, like to pump the heart, and...

"She says the tercet, the rhyme, me, to Nikki. In my voice."

No talking, for several minutes. Rex finished his dinner, then ordered his "usual". Troy let the waiter bus his uneaten meal.

Rex continued, "The instant the Romani hooker, uhhh, '*midwife's*' my truth, I gasp like I've been underwater for a year. I bolt upright. I'm in the city morgue. Three people are in the room, they all scream like little kids. One runs away. Another, takes my vitals, gibbering like Lou Costello in those horror comedies.

After my breathing and heart rate level out, I show normal on everything. I've got blood all over me, but they can't find any wounds. The bullets passed through, of course, but I'm not about to scoot on this one. X-rays, tests, interrogations. They hold me 'til 11:30 that night.

"Finally, the Chief of Police talks to my parents. Says he has no clue, but if this is a prank, I'll do 30 days, no good time. I don't know it yet, but Nik's already at home with a desk appearance ticket, gladly gonna plead to "illegal discharge of a firearm within city limits". The folks won't buy I'm not up to something. They want me to stay home from school. Right! I couldn't wait! Barely slept. Hot damn, I played it smooth all day. 'Huh? *Gunshot* wounds? *Yezz,* I have no idea what you're talking about.' It was my best day, Troy, the best day of my whole life."

Troy had to sip water at last. His throat was all frog. Ice cream cake was placed before the mayor, he of rubber and rhyme. And the special event went on.

"Of course, Nikki never came back. The rumors we heard, were nuts. But, Mr. and Mrs. Herrick were nuts, you know how they sheltered her when she was a kid, remember? They just fell back on old habits. No one's allowed in their house. Nikki's hardly ever seen. My buds and I, we used to do "Nikki sightings", made up lies about she'd been here or we saw her over there. I'm pretty sure that's how Lorna Jensen wound up in a padded room, the year after graduation. In wake of what happened and the Herricks being like they were, Nik got turned into some spooky zombie story. It was about there, you came in. I want to thank you for that, by the way, Troy. Serious. From my blackened heart."

The mayor fell to his cake, "mmm"ing at it. Troy watched the animal, overcome.

You made her a whore, and told the whole school. I saw girls pull their clothes away, to keep from touching her. You think it's made right with a blockful of dead bodies, a lick of egg money, and Thank You, Troy. She's dead, Rex. Dead human, living creature. Suffers every day. Condemned to wander the Earth, after I'm gone. There's no remedy for that, Rex. Because that bright, golden day in senior year, is water out to sea.

A bite of the chocolate, two bites of the white. More scotch. Rex laid fork aside.

"Naturally, I was never permitted to see her. I once suggested it to my Mom, and she hit me with a closed fist. *Jesus! That* never happened, before! I left off trying. Then, one night, it's around 3 in the morning, it's August. I leave for USC in another ten days. There's a dot of rain outside, not much. I can't sleep. I see a shadow at the window, figure it for a bud with some contraband. I get up, throw back a curtain.

"There stands Nichole.

"My room was at the back of the house, Troy. No streetlight penetrated. I came close to wigging out from insomnia, at USC. To this day, I use a sleep patch for my eyes. But there, that night, and with an 18-year-old's night vision, I still can't see her well, for the shadows...but, I know she's naked. I have no clue what this is about, but I'm squinting, darting looks to see if she has a gun. Nik doesn't talk for a long time, and the dripping turns into a real, soft summer rain.

"I don't know what to even say, but in my head, I'm seeing her through the Romani prostitute, and somewhere in there, I'm 9, again, and Pat's telling me the rhyme, so quiet. I'm staring at Nikki, at her forever-perfect body, as the rain falls, as it drops, comes down.

"Finally, Nik says in a voice kind of like mush, 'Well. You win. There is no justice in the world. Life was a bitch, and then, I died'."

"She steps back into the yard. I can see her better, now, and—my *God! Troy!* You think you got the short end, but you didn't. If some demon had handed me a burning parchment right then, my soul was his. *And* my complete set of Willie Mays cards.

"Nikki lifts her hands in a kind of lost, elder worship, like some nymph. A water elemental...and I get it, all at once. I understand, like the Romani host. Nik tilts her head to the stars, drinks from the falling rain.

"This is me, Rexford," she says. "This, is what you made. I'll be here ten thousand decades, live on after the last of your line. I won't ever try and kill you, again, but I hope you won't mind if I sometimes piss on your grave.

"And she dropped her hands and walked away, naked, into the dark. I went to the fridge and threw back four of my Dad's Coors. I never knew the whole schmear, until you called that first time."

Rex stared at his ice cream cake. Dabbed at it with a finger, tasting like a child. There remained no more to say, so typically, he said the exact, wrong thing.

"I loved her, Troy. I'm a bad, bad man, but once upon my youth, she was my god."

Troy pushed back from the table, and stood.

He said, "The monthly stipend, will be fine. I'll be by the car."

The plainclothesman was on the kitchen chair, weapon in hand. He nodded to Troy, handing him his keys on the way out. Troy headed to check the bathroom. He always secured a bit of colored yarn, which would fall should the door be interfered with. The yarn was in place, and Troy felt better. No one could see her like this, but him. That would be a real violation.

Troy stood by the tub, not opening the shower curtain. He talked to Nikki, like he'd talk to a cat. He told her almost everything that happened. He knew he'd have to repeat it, when she solidified. He just had to talk to someone, and Nikki was all he had.

The Xanax, holding stress merely steady, outside, rose up, sleep monster, shortly on. Troy lay down in bed, alone. He called good night down the hall. He told Nikki he loved her. He'd censored Rex's bit of confessional, at Ruhlin's. Nikki didn't need to hear that shit.

Soft pillow. Starless void of sleep. He dreamed. He was at the ocean. It sang, epic song, to him, possibilities endless, and he knew the ocean as Time. A buzzing insect, shiny blue jewel, zipped about near, far, back, gone, coy, coquettish, playing for his attention. The jewel, blue enough it looked ice in its own melt...Nichole's eyes?...was 1979. It tempted and teased. It said it wasn't lost, but always. *Catch me*, it said. *Catch me.*

Dive, a double gainer. Troy sank, lost and irredeemable in Time's ocean, and Nikki became that ocean. Troy drank and drank, filling himself with her. The pretty 1979, jewel in full melt, spun away. Troy drank in Nichole's infinity. He could hold her until he went into darkness, someday, filled of her wonder. Her's, but not his. Troy drank of endless, suffering beauty, wanting to call, implore the little jewel to return. Both what he had and hadn't, drowned him.

And he was on the school patio, screaming for the world to not leave, for Reality to make sense forever. Nikki clicked back the trigger, aiming dead on at their youth.

Boom. Boom.

Utter dark.

Troy came awake to warm arms and warmer lips. Nikki's tongue was in his mouth. She was wrapped around him, python. Best alarm clock in the world.

Nikki was solid in embrace, all-flesh and blood and human things. She was drop dead gorgeous, Troy's angel. His shining star. But for a couple inches off the top, Troy's baby was unchanged. Some person, some thing not battered ugly by cares of this world. Not scarred aged, by its coldness. Forty seven-year old seventeen year-old. Retro in organic relief. Right down to golden, feathered hair.

Troy noticed she was dressed—just an old tee and jean shorts, but Nichole's code for "touch me not". Troy didn't take this personally. Often, there was a lot on their plate. Nikki was good at running a household. She was good at a lot of things. Sad, she had missed out on living a life, but he never heard her complain. Possibly, being a walking, thinking myth, offered perspective.

They didn't need to speak. She smoothed his brow. Troy watched her face, mindful of what Rex had said. How it was he, Troy, who'd won. Such a thought, led only one direction. Troy's hands began to move. Nikki fielded them, expert, as they all learned by the time a guy got the guts to ask one out.

"Nono," she said. "I've got the bank, today, and the anniversary cake for my Mom. And you wanted that manuscript mailed Priority. The post office is a wait-and-a-half, remember?"

He stared, knowing the drill and hating it. Nichole, grateful for roof and his help always, threw a hand out, up, in theatrics.

"I'm with you, Troy...but, mundane life is busy life. And you with the Panic, and me..."

The sentence ended without ending. Just like her. She got out of bed and went to lean against the door jamb. Stretched. Yawned. Fluffing feathers of a jewel flown away.

"There's always a lot to get done," she explained, "and I only have so many hours. I love you...but lemme let *you* know, when I have time."

He grinned.

“Okay, sweets. How damned sorry can I be?”

Her 'smirk-smile'. A young shoulder, propelling from the jamb.

“Pretty sorry,” she said. “Gotta shower.”

“Nikki?”

Melting blue eyes, twin baby spots. Troy regarded her gaze with his own. He spoke softly.

“D...d'you still hate him? Rex? Hate him, for this 'you'?”

Her own stare was watchful. Nichole Herrick-Boland's eyes were in that minute, brimful with the pain Wisdom always jiggered into the shot. Wisdom and its cheap party buddies, Sadness and Defeat. There was always bile, sour, stagnant, in the wisdom of she who aged. Even if she didn't.

“All the time,” admitted the glue holding Troy's meager life in place. “Just, never first thing in the morning.”

Off to the shower, padding down the hall. Clothes discarded on the way, in manner of any good teen worth her excesses. Aphrodite from another Day, stepped into the shower, young and smooth and fresh and new. Troy heard the water, then felt the ubiquitous pain begin in both wrists. He cringed. Serious stuff, today. Maybe steer clear of computer work.

He stared at the ceiling, as one did on their sickbed. He turned head, seeing into the middle distance. He often wished he had killed Rex Cromwell, too. An accomplice, somehow. Troy used to think about that, all the time. 1979 for them both, instead of just her. The ultimate, physical law being, Pain Found You Out. Denial, meditation, philosophy—these, were pinwheels held crucifix, at monsoon. Growing old and dying, hurt. He would be old, soon enough, then gnarled, then hoary, then dead and in the ground. And Nikki would be alone, living water at flow in the night. All that suffering, for crumbs of years. Pacified by a literal mess of pottage.

From under water firing hard and hot, he heard Nikki, siren, calling snips of Steely Dan. Pressing crossed wrists hard in, mimicking a corpse, Troy thought about the newborn smell of 1979, and he cried.

The Special Units

Lt. Ammons considered the overgrowth, below. Thick, heavy grasses of the Alleghenies, obscuring insect, vermin. Anything small. Anything lying flat and silent.

Under a spreading chestnut tree, said grasses cresting above wheels, the stolen wagon. Mottle-brown gelding in harness, profile, docile. The pride of Ammons' commander, one ready Gatling gun, balanced so, in the wagon. Loaded, ammunition belt hanging, business end angled away. The horrifying firepower of what Captain Tell called, "the devastator", was not to fear.

The grass, was. There were You in it. Five, to their four men. The Rebels had surely sent all five.

They had made Red Candy Hill, more than a day before. Cherokees conscripted as intelligence, had Rebels coming in a direct line, the same road they had labored to find. The Union grouping, stragglers and survivors having combined through weeks in lost march, were pulling too much. Melting to forest again, was no good. The senior officer, default commander Captain Tell, elected to wait for the Confederates. To confer, under a flag of truce.

It hadn't been a rip-roaring success.

Late yesterday morning, Ammons had watched,

listening as Tell, flanked by guards, stood feet away from an older Rebel officer and his single protector, a Zouave whose colorful finery harkened to hole-y cheesecloth. The Rebs otherwise, were stopped as the road curved, below. Lt. Ammons didn't believe what he saw among their ranks.

The Rebs were fielding Antediluvian creatures. Biblical horrors unaccepted by any who even believed in them. Things thought lost in far centuries, deadly enough “rare” brought no comfort. A small menagerie of myths which should be in Hell or a bottle.

At right, shambling beside command, bursting its soiled uniform, a 12 foot Goliath. Ammons had been at study in Ypsilanti when the call to arms begged enlistment. Medical science and proven, said such heights could not stand or long live, due to gravity. Apparently, no one told this brute in white kepi and dirty neckcloth. Its shoulders were as wide as a chiffarobe, head level with the officer riding to the inside.

Above, forward center of what appeared a scarce unit, a she demon, a succubus, identifiable so in its shame. Great wings of bone and spike in leather, flapping lazy as it held back to stay with them. An unfurled battle flag, fringed, of slight tatter, hanging immense from sinewy arms, billowing. She was grinning.

And worse. Unimaginable. Leading, a trio of fife and drum at rest, flanked by soldiers their duplicates, left and right shoulder arms giving symmetry. All five impossibly the same person, not an angle different or curve, without blemish. Exact in height, shape. Impassive of countenance, machinelike in movement. Ammons had heard of the things--a supposed third being in Eden uncreated by God as superfluous ...these, didn't look uncreated or dead. "You", was the name of the pointless creation. Each was as the other, and as the original in Paradise, a neuter serving no useful purpose. Apparently, the Confederate States had found one: "legendary fodder"--the You, existing scrolls told, were those who "stood ready", lived in service. *How fitting:* Lt. Ammons, in rare pique, spat.

Captain Tell, acting commander following loss of superiors as the company wandered, descended the hill to midpoint with decorum. Rising to meet Tell and his guards, white flag of truce held aloft on his sabre, the Reb officer whom the Goliath had flanked. At his hip, the stiff, dirtied Zouave.

At several feet, both commanders halted in unison, saluting.

Cold formalism.

"Major Sanford A. Elmyre, at your service, officer."

"I am Captain Benjamin Jameson Tell, 11th Indiana, Grand Army of the Republic. So we might avoid useless, miniscule bloodletting, as both our groups be ragged bands, I would ask you, Major, to give us the road."

Pointed correction.

"As 'tis you who wait in full deployment, Blue Junior, it strains credulity you could not have made at least a day. Swerved, mannerly. We might never have met."

"You have more horses, Major, but we have more wagons," reasoned Tell. "I do not hold with abandoning goods I do not own. I waited for you."

Amused, one who would not be fooled.

"Mmm*yessz*, and well defended. We number but two score less four. Will you say your number and state what fear?"

"Fifty-five, but most handle goods, ordnance. The wagons. We're slow moving, in any event. And your three dozen, pardon riposte, sir...your count stated, excludes exotics, special units of the cursed Adamic World. I believe Jefferson Davis agreed these would ne'er be used afield."

Fast light in Elmyre's orbs.

"So, we are afield of one another! You admit this?"

Captain Tell, possessed of short fuse, hit his limit.

"You have a thirst, sir?"

"*I do, sir,*" said Elmyre though clenched good teeth, staring offended at Tell's own mouth. "And I shall petition your subject to President Davis, as he hangs upon the tree from which you butchers drape him!"

"Then, I will take leave of you, Johnny Major," said Tell, feigning heartiness to further get Elmyre's goat. "If you would only, sate curiosity: why do monsters and shades of Scripture, serve a Cause of bondage? I may guess well of your succubus, but a Goliath? A band of You! These, the banished, unwanted, driven into the wilderness! These, love the chains of others?"

"They are soldiers, sir," said Elmyre. "As my corporal and I (nodding at the hole-y Zouave, who blinked, cold).

They are in duty of service, and no distinction, they are paid."

Tell laughed aloud.

"No doubt in greenbacks," he rejoinder'd, then backing away, bayonets of protectors set *en garde* against the scandalized Major and his man.

Lt. Ammons saluted as the Captain neared.

"He's like them all, a vengeful coot's had his tea cozy stolen," said Tell, not returning salute, unlooking. "They'll be using the illegal things. To arms!"

"To arms! To arms!" called Ammons, and he left mind pictures to again stare down upon the grasses. Thicker, underneath the wagon. Thicker, around the spreading tree.

Yes, no doubt. All five sent to guard the prize thieved. The Gatling was holy terror to utilize; men had gibbered in steadying, emoted as children. Its roar of bullet-spit, made Ammons consider the mouth of God Himself and judgment upon stupid Man. Red Candy Hill, were it not for the rogue piece, would be thrice red from Union blood. Rebs fought mad unto dying, for their dying way.

The devastator was found gone immediate, in morning's light. It had proven so monstrous, even slaying in grotesquery a monster of theirs', the bluecoats had been certain all was settled; that the Major in gray elected "to the end", was disgusting, no more. The Gatling and enough schooled to use her, was trump card. It, its wagon re-hitched to the placid gelding, had in darkness, been led away. The nearest guard's throat was cut, by what a conscript from Western territory deemed, "Indian bone". The You. However wronged in Eden, modern descendants didn't forgive.

They were experts, crawling on their bellies...papyri hinted they had existed to protect Man, this a bit illogical, before The Fall. They could slither, and faster than any serpent. Ammons had seen bone daggers kill, seen them divide dinner, expert, beside campfire. He had been dispatched with three men, a German paid to replace unwilling gentry in ranks, and two other privates, one frightened, one angry. The angry one, Tayman, was on tether, primed...the other, grown out of being boy fifer at war's declaration, was "Doodle", saucer eyes as dreading as Tayman's were grim. The German, Otto Schacht, in European acceptance, only waited.

Again, Ammons flashed on Ypsilanti, a point to argue in Logic: the You, assassins unseen, might be taken out by concentrated fire, but a quartet of barrels was not enough, a game of dice, blind odds steep. Only the Gatling would spread a carpet quickly enough to slay, and the Gatling was the weapon sought. Maddening!

Captain Tell, would be unaccepting, of any insoluble problem. Ammons had once heard his superior growl to a wagoner, "By God, break it off and *make* it fit!" No matter their lives, the whole point of war said, "the goal, supersedes blood". The lieutenant, having stepped down far enough the slope to judge depth of the grass sea, had an idea he did not like. Looking back as he sought to rejoin them, he saw in Doodle's eyes, a child's "*Please?*" Ammons understood...but judgments of Scripture, governments or commanders in the field, told. Your fear, was the last thing to be considered.

Yesterday, in hottest afternoon, fear was a tundra, chilling all around. The Rebels, as dancers aligning formal, moved to advance position with haste. The GAR readied for them. Mixed and ragtag, their scouts few, Tell had stayed at the men. Drills as able, especially when weather halted their wandering. Tell held even the marching order set for rapid deployment—here, the Rebel Major so itching for a fight, called their waiting what it was. The unit joined too, as dancers for a reel. Each, with fantastic timing, in perfect place. The Captain stood close to his tent. Both sharpshooters and the flying platoon plead him back. But for Ammons, no other officer was present in ranks, and after previous losses, all feared for Tell. They said he could not be risked. This led to the surprise of Ammons' week.

"Get you up top," Tell ordered as the lieutenant neared his side. "Assist Mister Shronke. Ready the Gatling. I'll command for 'the net'."

Rapidly blinking, the lieutenant on heel spun away. The found weapon and its nursemaid were out of place at the crest of Red Candy Hill, but Tell believed a clear field looked down upon, would aid the deadly magicks of their unique gun.

It was fog o' war and a bit of Fate the unit had this scythe of a battery. The Gatling was rare, something very new. The GAR wasn't known to have secured any, though Ammons heard tales from their expert found, lone survivor guarding it, hidden near dead horses and men, in a West Virginia barn.

Nels Schronke, a small man of white sideburns, was not young but spry, and bandy-legged. Schronke, was teacher of the Gatling's handling. He'd held extended talks, demonstrated hands on. Any who wished to learn the weapon, could now crew if but they obeyed—Schronke was long busted to buck private, yet everyone beside Tell, called him, “sir”.

Further underscoring his point about “a clear field”, Captain Tell had kept the Gatling anchored in the wagon where it first had been unlimbered. It sat higher than anything afield. Given line of sight, it had terrible power. Mr. Schronke was puttering, checking connections. Making certain the ammo belt had free flow. Lt. Ammons looked about for further support—three could cope with the ungainly technology, though four were preferable. He summoned a couple of enlisted via hand signals, and was up into the wagon behind shortest side panels. The horse was unhitched, standing protected by blessed blinders, downwind, feet distant.

“Expect this insurrection, to shovel us unholy nightmares,” Ammons commented as they rechecked. “This cannon of bullets is fearsome, but at the least of Man and the Army's own trust!”

An amused grunt. Schronke shook head, still bent, hard at work.

"Thiz'z no more regulation'n them Antediluvians," he said, puffing a bit. "This one come outta Pittsburgh. The Penn Guard was puttin' down a strike. Paid 'em well, Mr. Ammons, sir. We paid 'em well."

"Who paid them?" asked Ammons, uncomfortable now as he was glad for the gun.

"Chain a' command, young Mr. Ammons. We're here a mashed up group, hard bits clung to a plate. Not a face famous, not Sherman, not Grant, not Meade would care but more butternut nuts's laid down. If it helps, you steady to guide. I'll fire."

Ammons wanted to respond, *We'll need more than us*, but the pair just bidden were up and into position as anchormen, leaving Ammons sole privilege to feed the heavy belt. Schronke fast reminded one of the men, the meaning of "steady". Metal clicks and clinking of all manner--the new gun, its belt, spurs of one enlisted man making song, guns near, readied..."plinks" and hollow "clacks", tapping, metal, and metal to clash. The sword of only defense, conqueror versus conqueror in protection...

That first day's battle, one of tired ire presented by commanders, decided nothing. It should have. It did not. Never short of zeal, on call of bugles by three of the You, statuary in a theater's placard, the Rebs advanced upward as the flying platoon fired and backed. Captain Tell in winking, had versed all riflemen in affecting fear, reforming. He had organized them as for improvisation—this one to drop his weapon and abandon it nearest the rear, that one to slip and quake on reload. Two more thought loud of mouths, to cry out. And these and those to mark one target apiece, to bring it down. The platoon on third reform backward, were here to fade, ground's edges, as a large net, against trees and wagons and rock. There was sparse ordnance, for hand—those who stood better with pistol, were not to reload rifles, but drop and draw. "As dueling," Tell framed it. "Mark the dishonorable, and use every chamber."

The Rebs had fallen for it, beautifully, but their special units obeyed no rules. The demoness, caught in belly and wing, threw battle flag with pole as javelin, it lit in standard bright fire from nowhere. It struck a man dead against a wagon wheel, and the single cannon to the Gray rear, blew the wagon shattered, with shell. The You, fast and disappearing through confusion of their number, lit upon men too far forward, and like cannibals, sank perfect teeth, school bullies—whereupon partners arose, one further hamstringing, another assassin by bone dagger. Several Union men were fast silenced by this murder, then one more, and the You were gone, vanished.

The Goliath, charging forward in great strides, hefting a man high and punching him dead, was a battalion of one. The Gatling's triumph, hailed later by Tell, was focused on him. Bursts first to slow and cripple--then, as saviors for him targeted Schronke and crew, these were picked away by sharpshooters. The mean roaring gun shot the huge beast and shot it. The Goliath, halted through lower damage, held forth his blood, in agony leering them belittlement. Red hands begged more. The species' hate, was clear; the blue men were ants and less. Mister Schronke called it a name in Swedish, and Ammons felt the Gatling clatter on tripod as the monster was blasted gone. A Union enlisted barely rolled out from under to safety, as the Goliath, laughing claret, fell back.

Ammons could see Elmyre, as at practice, firing cool where Tell must be; the lieutenant assumed his Captain fired in like. The flying succubus, seeing capability of the gun, dove, screaming. She was expert, in angle; they could not elevate it, sufficiently. Just then, Tell was around from his tent, spinning into clear, going to one knee. He caught the thing, twice—wing-claw, ear. The leathered killer spun to spy him, and Captain Tell cursed her, rising, extending aim. Gargling revenge, the succubus was fast away.

The Rebs, having shot their proverbial bolt, were retreating. At least ten lay dead, perhaps more. The Goliath, was vanquished, the flying demon, wounded. Union wagons had splintered from the far-off cannon; the grays must field crack artillerymen. Only seven GAR dead, but more than twice, wounded—the guerrilla tactics of the special units, had hobbled many. Seeing firsthand the Gatling gun's wanton shredding of not just the Goliath, but “mowing a bit of a Confederate field”, Tell felt confident the matter decided. Alone, he and Elmyre stood each beneath white upon sword tips, before dusk. After several minutes, Tell watched the Rebel officer downhill, then returned bearing a look of bewilderment.

"My father was with General Scott, in Texas," he told a circling of them. "I heard from him, the tales we know of the Alamo's defenders, are truth. I never thought that could be a bad stubbornness. Get food and sleep. The wild men come again, tomorrow."

A Cherokee scout reported in midmorning. Elmyre had 2nd day's attack set for last of daylight. For all his honor and being 'the wronged', the Rebel commander did not concern himself with tradition. As Schronke called them "butternut nuts", the Confederate major saw it reversed: the GAR were crazed, all mad killers...and they were in his way. Captain Tell said the Major was frothing, on that subject.

If not for the theft in morning's dark, combining rude trick of late attack, the five creatures would not be here. But You in deep grass, stripped to Nature in aid of concealment, froze it. They were there, of course, but Ammons' group could exhaust ammunition, rube stolen blind at a carnival...and a fool or four whole fools, would have feet and ankles sliced and chopped, calling "bluff!" They were needed as much as the Gatling, but Tell would cry blue murder at even this excuse. The Union had won the first day; counting on fingers, the grays couldn't have but two dozen men remaining. The horrific Goliath, was fallen. But, Tell...he loved the Hell gun too much. Ammons fancied the Captain wanted to marry it.

They stood in counsel, on the hill before the grasses. Beneath, under chestnut's chorus of branches, the gelding and its wagon of trophy, pretty as in a locket, shared. Wanting more men, better men and enemy men instead of impossible creatures, his lone, dark epiphany brought Ammons' group no comfort.

"Three of us, backs in, a triangle, shoulders touching," the Lieutenant found himself saying, jaws dropping from all. "Bayonets, only. Concentrate as if neither comrade could help you. The fourth, sharpshooter, sat higher up, near."

Otto Schacht, oiled moustache a double bladed knife out to there, in half-good English requested position of shooter. Hand to hand with monsters flat to ground, wasn't popular with poor Doodle.

"Sharp's repeaters, in'na ordnance wagon," he offered.

Ammons shook head. "Waste of daylight. If they rise up, bayonets work in frenzy. No man has cool aim, suddenly lit on."

"I'm ready," said Tayman, eyes ever angry. Face, grim.

"Otto, you're sharpshooter," Ammons nodded to the German. "Highest ground. Fire best approximation, no matter us."

"*Jawohl, Herr Leutnant.*"

Confidence was not boosted as they watched him double time, uphill.

"Shoulder to shoulder to shoulder," Ammons ordered, quiet, intense. "I'm always top point. Ready arms."

They prepared, then settling into their triangle, tight. It might have been a party game, laughter about, and gaiety. The wind, was the world's only sound. Ammons, who carried a mammoth Colt's Dragoon, locked back its trigger.

"With my guidance...at the half-step...*advance...*"

And down, into natural American mountain's jungle. Green, a crinkling of holiday tissue, sang. It waved, serpent's buzz in beat of dance, all around.

The thick, high grass deep in, was swamp, wetting socks, trousers. Ammons, feeling them push, some boys' competition, stayed deliberately slow. He could see the wagon in upper periphery, mirage of welcome. Inner tingling, stopping them quarter seconds, when loomed a sizable insect. No reports from the enlisted; Doodle made noises in his throat. The Dragoon had great heft, a fine boulder in Ammons' hand.

The officer focused, straight line drawn, adjusting as needed. Though he could sense Doodle glancing, mad, toward weathervane Otto, the others were feel, only. Unneeded, unwanted creations, somewhere beneath. Stories returning, from childhood. A supposed "Book of Hezekiah", killed at Nicea from inclusion to Scripture, which "spake of that not, at conclusion, desired". Depiction of Adam and Eve as tormentors, uncaring. The little thing of no gender, appealing to YHWH. The little thing itself, decided as problem. *But it was assumed away. How is it here, in league with slaveowners, usurpers? "I am angry"? "I will strike back"?* Again, the Goliath in mindseye, inn's rude miscreant full of drink. Blood drenched, asking metal better's fire. Dying, for why? As why it lived, anyway?

By ten steps past midway, breaths of terror began

faster as gasps of hope. The last thirty paces, the shoulders of the enlisted were pushing. Ammons had his Dragoon steadied using both hands, gripping the barrel. Aimed now underneath the wagon. Swallowing his breath. Grasses and weeds still passing in rustle. Bobbing, land ocean.

"Otto's wavin' his kepi!" cried Doodle, little boy. "We have to be there!"

"...and five more, four, three," counted Ammons, then, "Up into it! Leg!"

He spun in a roll around Tayman, who pushed to the inside, and both the boys were laughing, campfire tale to tell, jumping, up, pulling into wooden safety. The Lieutenant's lead foot was on the toe board. He legged into the spring seat, troubled by this ease.

A heavy carbine report, too near. The mottle brown in full harness emoted, bolting. Ammons reached, quick, for the reins, but the gelding's trace dropped as nothing, to the ground; on the unseen side, there was none. A veiled illusion. The horse hadn't been held, to start. The animal ran, picking up speed, leather lines floating ribbons. Both privates, lamented.

The tableau stole precious seconds they might have discerned smoke to track the shot. They'd not been targeted. More sinister...for a glance to high ground, showed no one. The German as any soldier, would scarce have abandoned his position. Otto Schacht wasn't there, because Otto wasn't anywhere.

No covering fire remained. No transport back. Just they three. Without provisions. In company of a Gatling which couldn't be depressed in fire but so low, and Rebel-loyal You, outnumbering. Ammons looked to the sun. Perhaps two hours, before the sky commenced to dim. Ammons knew the You would stay. No pure play was upon their minds, but blues' own mind play, imprisoning. No simple guard duty, "watching over". Not control with mercy. Things pushed away by very God, whatever current beliefs husbanded, would strike fast, if panic, or wait for drowsiness. For sleep.

Tayman, Doodle, looked to him. For a short while, they said nothing. The lieutenant's own silence, one of thinking without result, told them. Doodle, the manchild. Each came after a time, to see the pickle a game of strategy, mental puzzle. Moving things, without loss. There was too much tension for study. Ammons bade them nap for night watch, before stress could again draw tears or worse.

As time passed, at every opening without syllable or human noise, Ammons inclined hearing. To directly beneath them. Unable to ramify the Rebel Major's reasoning. Things of Old, were without calculation. These, had stardeep reasons. Pain from a Sand Earth. Who could understand? Confederate dollars, Federal, gold pieces, crown jewels... Army officers, men of results, demanded cause and effect. For special, Antediluvian units, it was what sat in a cryptic glyph. One looked, then knew. Feeling beyond experience. That which was, and that not. "They are paid", indeed. Yes, but as Schronke said. The Gatling, too deadly, paid their Goliath, well. Ammons considered the heavy tarpaulin yester eve, draping the Southern dead. Near-tented, for the Goliath, within.

The lieutenant reflected on him, the You. The demon female. America, was so young. The world of the Pharaohs, of Christ and Moses, Antiquities and everything made which was made. Things not gone away, had come here with Columbus, the Dutch, the French, with the East India Company and the starving Irish...now, the Germans. From every land, slipped that unwanted or thought left behind. Goliaths. Methuselahs. Demon folk. The You, not uncreated after all. And Man of 1864 went about knowing, constantly afraid. Only Law, would make things to vanish. Or, Matthew Brady's celebrated camera...after all, if eventually no one *saw*...

Lightest shadows, began. In harmony with silence, the officer only ever detected a hint of battle from that direction. The conflict, now weighting more in favor of the Rebels, felt of failure. He couldn't care about that. None would likely care about them.

After a time, the checkmated lieutenant tilted head back, pushing cap's visor further with thumb. He considered their gift of shade, the great chestnut. As structure, system. A community of branches. Chestnut trees, were glory; their grain was perfect and straight--Ammons had seen. He marveled, nodding at the orchestration of leaves on the wind. Their shelter as such, was a very good tree.

A MESS O´ VISITORS

Rochelle's supervisor at Quantico, came off "dress parade"; he even readjusted her pant cuffs. Grave, in first day's briefing. Emphasizing they worked sanitation, clean up. If she liked, "environmental". They were janitors. Earth was lethal flypaper. A helpful thing, but messy. A dirty job. Perhaps noble. Lucrative. *Do the work.*

Their craft, a radically modernized Tilting Duct V/STOL, rose vertically on 4 shaft turbines--then, with speed of the old Concorde, shot forward. Rochelle had graduated the Air Force Academy. The STOL wasn't for everyone. The supervisor played with speeds and altitudes for the first half hour. Seeing her unbothered, he relaxed into informality. "Randon", was easy company. Focused, efficient work, he advised. Past that, he was "kick it guy".

Northern Vermont. The STOL set down in a clearing uphill from a flowing creekbed. A diminutive spacecraft had been scuttled. Burnt hollow. Abandoned. Randon said they'd never find survivors. Woodland creatures being territorial, etc.

"There's legions of roadkill," he said, as they pulled the blackened, toy-size hull from mud. "Any vessel has a limited complement."

The ship was light as styrofoam. They carried the

wreckage uphill. Rochelle eyed it.

"'Looks like that Civil War ship. The Merrimac?"

Her supervisor grunted.

"Kind of appropriate, then. The crew torching it and splitting."

"Why?" asked Rochelle, unsteady as the ship's central fusion rocket broke off in her hand.

"The Merrimac's crew did the same thing, once she proved a piece of shit."

The hulk went into the STOL's hold. Rochelle extended the broken piece, apologizing. Randon cavalierly tossed it in.

Southern Illinois. A lot of rainfall made the job dicy. A spidery ship, deployed opened as land crawler, draped over some kid's high treehouse. After twenty minutes trying to pull from all angles without harming the structure, Rochelle was ordered to flip it free. They landed, loaded, made cursory check of immediate ground, and continued West. Sweeping up shards of Visitors exploded onto Beartooth Highway 212 in Wyoming, despite elevation, was a knee jerk.

Lunch, was on the government. They ate Elvis' favorite, fried peanut butter, bacon and banana sandwiches, in Denver. Cane sugared sodas. Talked sports, climate change. Then just southwest, near Leadville. A half-melted "Oofoh", as Randon called wrecks, needing scraped from a canyon wall. Rochelle, gas mask employed against rot of alien dead, had scut duty. Randon kept the STOL immobile as could, inches from the cliff. Materials of this race were sticky, resistant. Bits of vessel and casualties at intervals dropped to canyon's floor. Policing, made the job twice as long. It was past 1500 hours, before they reached the Mojave desert.

Many tiny dead, shadowed by cacti. Those "other properties" of distant stars: they were flashfrozen. Refrigerated, in Sol's glare. This race, Randon recognized as refugees. They kept trying, never learning.

Rochelle used an outdoor industrial vacuum. Randon bagged select corpses in a stenciled canvas sack, inspecting each as one would fruit, for discoloration. She noted the stenciling read "EATS", and gulped.

"The size of these races," Rochelle remarked, buckling in. "It's like the whole universe is *Gulliver's Travels*!"

"We're fortunate Earth's atmospheric properties smash crap outta everything," was Randon's response. "Tech wins, and we suck. Minus Nature, we're long ago toast."

She knew the drill. He recited, anyway.

"No spacecraft, survives entry to Terra Firma. Through recorded history, they've bellied down, bottomed out, hit nose first, exploded, imploded, disintegrated to mist... Any landing, asphyxiate, flashfreeze, spontaneously combust, whatever. Me, I figure Earth has a big 'GO AWAY' cut into the Himalayas."

"The foundation has secured all floors," intoned Rochelle, proper air of solemnity. "If we mock with fear, we stand in doubt."

Randon glanced several times before asking, "You religious?"

"My adoptive parents were," she answered. "They said Earth, 'our home', was only for us."

"Huh. I wanta argue, but it's hard."

"I know. Everything we're cleaning up."

"Yeah," said Randon. "Not even allowed by atmosphere! So...I guess that's part of it..."

Return to HQ, was by way of New York. Urban cleanups, rare, were a different department. Randon said there was a confirmation, in Bedford-Stuyvesant. Rochelle narrowed eyes.

"No Oofoh's going to *not* be noticed, in NYC."

"A crash wouldn't," he replied. "This is Meals on Wheels."

The STOL was sat down atop an abandoned parking garage. Rochelle also got out, but was ordered to hang back. Randon, canvas bag in hand, walked down a ramp. Below, against a concrete pillar under graffiti, sat someone in rags. Hooded cloak. Knees drawn up, head bowed. Fetal. Rochelle came as far as the ramp, near distant.

The person began defensive posture. Randon presented the bag, displaying "EATS".

"I am worker," he said. "Some fuel-food crashed, again."

Hood pulled back. A complex android, feminine mocking. Left eye socket empty, charred. Synthetic facial skin shredded at left, nostril to crown. Pallid, stick fingers, human appearing, received the "EATS" bag. Randon respectfully requested "thanks".

The mutilated face tilted, angling best its one eye. Processing. Impassive.

"You're sports." A statement.

"Championship of Texas, next Sunday. The line says Houston, giving 2."

Distant approximation of a glaring smile.

"Off scale. Final score, 16-3, Cowboys. Defense holds the line. Offer Houston and 11, maximum coverable. Please do not retire. I am dependent on benefactors."

Randon kept a game face. He felt sorry for any who'd made it, existing stranded. Their aloneness. He nodded, stepping back, and the disfigured alien again shrouded her face.

The two-person crew didn't speak until halfway to Quantico. Rochelle cleared her throat.

"The revealed robotics. Crash survivor?"

"She's called Dec-El-Doh...and, no. 'Damage is courtesy of an outdated minigun mop ups employed. Camou dudes, Area 51-approved. 'Doesn't mean they're professionals."

Rochelle returned, "She's a hardy Visitor, anyway. Our size."

"She's a vessel. Her kind are their own ships. The dudes who goofed mop up, left her a century of hide and seek. The wrecked eye? Past the exosphere, guidance is hopeless. She's gotta wait 'til we reach her tech level and parts become commercially available. A good 72 years to go."

"That sports line...she's an AI oracle."

"I know," said Randon. "Another reason she's homeless, 'lost' in New York."

"I think her snack people are better off," said Rochelle, and he was silent.

They made HQ, spent serious time in paperwork, changed into street clothes and punched out. Before exiting, the supervisor asked Rochelle if the realities that first day had shaken her.

"Anyone growing up since the Internet, figures lots of 'Out There' is true," she said. "The masses just don't know details. Those details, are sad. Invaders or refugees, it's always about the pursuit of happiness. I'm catching on, why barely anyone wins that race."

Randon raised eyebrows. Smiled, small.

"In other words, it shook you up," he said. "The right way, maybe. See you at 0700 for pre-flight briefing."

The Realities of Cylinder Reversal

"They can only get the sled in so far! Drifts'r too heavy!"

The deputy's voice too, cut only so well into the winter wind. Another bad night was on deck. The bodies could be easily left. The sheriff even wanted to leave them. It wasn't duty, however, which forced his hand.

From much closer, "There's no way we have a body bag for two, Sheriff. These, are clamped in freeze! We have to steady as we haul 'em up. Whatta we do?"

Horn Matheson, coat collar clamped by hand over nose and mouth so close in to the corpses, did not look away from them as he answered.

"Improvise, Lucian. Get the tarp out 'back a' your car. It's big enough, we'll jellyroll 'em in."

"Yessir."

One step taken away, then, leaning back:

"Won't jostlin' 'em break off the, uhm...th'um..."

Matheson now looked up, wider of eye.

"'Take thawed out, before that breaks," he said. "What do you know about the *'th'um*?"

"Gram on Mom's side, kept witch company," replied Lucian. "Took a long time dyin', did some talkin'."

"Go do some doin'," the sheriff ordered, and the deputy was in hotfoot up the drifts.

Matheson was left alone with the starcrossed victims. Pia Roeffel, county vagrant, creature of need, and sad old Chelm Kinde, same. Both, emptiness as people, human spaces impossible to fill. Both, inmates of mental wards at one time, though Kinde's was so far back, it became but urban legend. Two people, cut off from others, skulking, lurching around. They knew each other. Spurned one another. Macy vs. Gimbel. Kinde had told him five years back, "She's working my side of the street!" Sheriff Matheson had noted, and throughout life, the antipathy each mentally ill person had for all others. Proper closure, perhaps, a mile from Kinde's car the two had died, wrapped as in passion, knives buried in one another, half submerged in a shallow rockbed stream.

Cursory inspection, showed a suicide pact. The expressions as partially visible, gratitude. "*Thank You.*" Loving. The act would have occurred before the fast freeze and snow dump, near-seamless. More than two days now, but the cold snap, extreme, preserved museum-like, slowing decomposition. The poor souls, an ice sculpture, looked only as in pallor mortis. As though it all went down within the hour instead of two days back. No animals had struggled through drifts to feed. Horrific mannequins, grey-waxen perfection. The awkward hug, pressing sightless eye to eye. Deputy Lucian Morrell's "th'um".

The eyeballs, fixed in delighted communion as a parent might play a silly game with baby or lovers express affection, showed alarmingly alive. Glorying, each, into the other. Pia's autumn gold and Kinde's somber brown, as flowering plants of lush summer, feeding one another with reciprocated gaze. Its utter affirmation. Eyes of both, only those close in the semi-hug, eyes of life, its fulfilling. Locked warm, feeding, existing beyond bodies or brains. And reactive at least, to light. Matheson, upon testing, had about shit his pants.

He could hear the boys from the Coroner's, hear Lucian acting as Scout Leader, and Matheson stood, creaking, never looking away from the fascinated mutual stare. Two sad lost ones, burying differences through agreed sacrifice. With continued lock on of sentient sight which, godstruck, beheld only its sustaining balance. Kinde, a thorough man, a planner, no doubt had calculated, re: the weather forecast. It was an accident the bodies had been found prior to Spring. Of course, where they were, having put themselves, untold millennia had passed. The Sheriff regretted his duty. He didn't know he regretted it awfully. The "th'um", known in Mason County, Illinois lore as a "spiritual cylinder", a forced collision through mutual absorption just as Death overtook, was supposedly ever done with right eyes locked in gaze. The vagrant girl and sad old tapper, were locked in lefts. Horn Matheson, for all he'd learned in 68 years of his strange Illinois locale, wasn't certain that mattered. It probably did.

The place was an ever-cascading corkscrew of bare, unnourished rock. For aeons, epochs, milliards of dimensional time, there had been only mist, a bath of it as All, a suffocation, and hot. Hot mist as flame, humidity as murderer's weapon. This mist grew tepid over unmeasured, uncountable reckoning, and the colder it grew, without wind it cried. A beam, as some divine flashlight would at once seek to penetrate, but the thick mist which ramped to eventual torrents of rain, was a wall. It existed, creature with back turned, seeking only to hide. That it grew colder and wept as itself, was not acceptance, but sleep. A sinking to dormancy. One kind of power, to reemerge as another.

Eventually, there became the proverbial bottomless pit of jagged, unforgiving rock wet by the rain, drenched of it, bathed in, forever cleansed but unaccepting. The mountainous corkscrew existed wet and dry and beat upon and resistant, all at once. This monstrous tunnel bearing incessant, unhelpful rains, was the diameter of a formed planet, a place too big for terrestrial life, but not sporting the pretentions of a gas giant. The tunnel fixed, set; waters once hard mist steaming, were cold, alone, a wrongturned creation. A nonplanet, malformed. The rain which could not help, long chilled. There was no more weeping. Wet untouching, pouring oceans through the solid hole, it kept a watch. The rock, without, was a mold. Within, silent oven.

This moment of Creation existed unchanged, without hope of tabulation, in a space without relation to Human or Earth.

The hill tilted to a crest because of the snow. The drifts were worse than they would have been; the man from Parks & Rec who'd come assisting, had illadvisedly tried to cut a path with a curling broom. The bottom level of snow, to then still wet, had iced. Sheriff, deputy and two more, slipped, dug in, slid. Horn Matheson cursed in five directions.

The tarp, purest vulcanized rubber, hung open underneath to a side. The wind above, whipped it away at intervals. The sun was sinking in slow fall, but the fix of the visual cylinder, reversed or not, gleamed. The light of living eyes, a fair-eternal lock, shown golden glaze. Laser-intense, more so by the dimming minute. Sheriff Matheson kept ordering and cursing, running his mouth—he had the side betraying the truth, and didn't care to discuss it. Deputy Morrell, through careful delegation, was on the same side of the sled, but positioned ahead. Ironic, that, and sneaky of the Sheriff, but though Lucian would hold his peace in the moment, he'd want to discuss it later. Hat in hand, like a shavetail asking for Musial's autograph. *No way.*

Pushing, shouting. The sled, fishtailing. A salient moment from *Fitzcarraldo*, the bow going higher, singing to God, totem, idol risen by slave multitudes. Hanging there, Matheson's voice Ahab in the wind, the stiff couple bound but tipping. Seconds, and the other lead man, Lucian in kind dragging down, powering straight on. Strong Man stuff. The sled fell forward, and Matheson went to both knees, scrambling up at once. Ahead, as they pierced in full evening, brights of the

Coroner's wagon. Quickly, the bay was opened. Groans. Excrement words. Breaths, producing a hearth's vapor.

The cylinder, a spiral, was grown to bluehot. Matheson knew movement was sensed. Bad enough. The night's cold was a dead one, hitting past garments and tarpaulins. There could be nothing else discernible. But scraps from Antiquity, were seldom detailed.

There came to be irregular day and night. Times of light were cold, a stiff breeze, its sound, only. The stone corkscrew as cut by endless gales, was pink and tan, both washed out, melded. Grasses, sparse and few, existed now. They stuck out, grasping knives.

The night, longer each duration, was presence. A wall, as the ancient mist, but with movement. Feminine of face, the mind might conceive. Turning. Looking ever backward, anticipating. Slowly, it turned, a wheeling of centuries, Enemy found backward, in reverse, 180. Night, in anthropological spin, defensive, of Time. The night was defender against all forcing it, molding into itself. Turning its feminine face, ageless. Judging what judged its essence. It knew what was behind, could almost see. What was gone, was never there and always there. All, as in this place, had never presumed. Behind, force stronger had decided, presuming. Making, editing. Past a point once more endless, the night began leaving sounds of pain, to growl.

On those mornings for the short space it came, the ever-rock, corkscrew more dense, more burnished, no longer touched by waterfalls of rain beginning slower, seemed to tumble as revolving, readying. Showing support. All here, intelligence--a Do, for Enemy had not let it Be. Fixed as in a crystal globe, this Reality was selfaware.

The caravan was pulling onto the main road. The Coroner's wagon had stuck on a bubble light, revolving red, authorized by the Sheriff. Even with sublime conditions, the deep freeze in their basement was 15 miles and more hamhanded lugging, away. This County had no budget for niceties like a van's contained bay with temperature control.

Deputy Morrell motioned him to stop as Matheson backed to follow. The sheriff rolled eyes, not bothering with the window, cracking open his door on the fly.

He said, "You gonna ask 'do I need you', yes. Only direct' official personnel, to the Coroner's. Watch it, but step on it."

Hand to hat as the wind picked up, Morrell asked, "Late work? I gotta call Brenda, if!"

"You can chittychat all night, but it's a long shift, Lucian," his superior told him. "And you'll receive instruction, but I ain't gonna tell you no ghost story."

#CLUNK#. Matheson snatched the driver door closed and waved a pointing finger at the Deputy's cruiser, backing quickly.

Lucian Morrell paused before sliding into his own car. He watched his fellows receding up the road to town, still pressing down his hat in the harsh wind. A final glance into far forest black, wondering after the "suicide pact". The "cylinder" Gram had told him of, as though upon her final rest she sought to spook him. Those two vagabonds, always convinced people were cruel. The Sheriff, unwilling to talk, so clearly in a hurry.

"*Goddam*," he muttered. Mad at himself. He had a personal day he'd almost used. Now, this. Bad shit, of which he knew a hunk. Overtime, saluting a man who kept his own counsel. But that known hunk, was the worst.

He responded on the Police Channel as prompted. *Roger that, pulling out, over.* Goosed the pedal, cavalier, to swing the car as he hit the road. Okay, yeah, suicide pact, no question. But only because you had to die to kick the thing off.

The mist permeated, cold smoke; the endlessness of immense valley, its vee crowded with lumpen green forest. A forest of stone.

The mist, heavy, always controlling, was spirit, essence strengthening in control. Finally risen as ever-covering, it spoke to the valley stretching on, perpetual, and the valley spoke back. They in empathy, far deep silent connection, took counsel. Each at core, "am", "is", first cell of beginning, knew the Other. Existing in purpose. Mutually restraining. The mist's rear, behind, blackened, was Before. Perdition and pain escaped, no longer able to touch. Yet, it had once touched. Universal mind in deepest communion searched, disseminated.

Looked at each component. Study by that flawed, yielded flawed study. Reality, creation, being, intelligence thereof, held only beginning ingredients. “Growth”, meant expansion. “Expansion”, meant strengthening. “Strength”, meant power. “Power”, meant this power was required...the 'why' of this, was the inherent flaw, introduced by harm. Before.

The cold vapor could only look upon the vast stone life, they in embrace of solidarity. This level of becoming, appearing still a mutant planetoid, shaped as spatial line, wide. Not as seen from a camera, sitting, not vista. The vee of hard, growing green, shielded by screen of mist, stood upright. No wall, but a battery. Not buttress, but array. Readying. Growth, expansion, strength, power. Behind cold, dense protector, in dark, existed Enemy. As an aeon gave way to another, the flawed, high finitude, continued to evolve. Never healing.

Even given the wide staircase down, high ceiling, elbow room, the barrel of two bodies, tarp forever falling open, was ungainly. The group stumbled. Staggered, in shifting. The Coroner, if new and young, strangled for air at the ground level. The Sheriff called Deputy Morrell a rank name, for leaving to dash up and close the entrance door.

All of them panting, three of them redfaced, pushed the solid statues stiff and blued, deep to freezer's rear. It was a holding for cadavers near-a century old, installed for convenience by craftsmen. A rumor existed the large freezer tank was constructed in expectation of Capone's men starting a hot war, over his incarceration. Mason County had hosted a few names, in The Past. Mason County was known for triple helpings of weird...too, it had tellers of tales. Yarns. The freezer, with only two other inhabitants, could have otherwise hosted a dinner party. Knowledge acquired through his many terms had Sheriff Matheson directing the position of the large gurney, to where he knew to be the coldest place in the room. Without ceasing movement or allowing anyone to decompress, Matheson shielded the living connection, eye cylinder now flavoring transparent colored spots, in one quick movement. Only Lucian Morrell had seen the cylinder, and he was needed, much as that stank.

Loose chat outside the holding area, a speck of paperwork talk. The much older Sheriff patting the exhausted Coroner on the back, asking after his health. Lucian on the cell with his wife, apologetic, lovey-dovey, suddenly stalwart as they all began to look. The assistant, passing a flask. Everyone had a few gulps. Matheson, knowing he had to stay razor, stopped with one.

With unneeded permission, Sheriff and Deputy were granted all night access to rest in the heated offices. These were upstairs by another route. Only to get all the feeling back, hearty acceptance. After some minutes on particulars, those medical let themselves out.

"Come back early or late," said Matheson to the

Coroner, who looked worn to tatters. “The cadavers'll just shift and roll away from one'n 'nother. Trust me.”

And the others were gone. The building was old, but the steam heat upstairs was mother's milk. Horn Matheson was opening his jacket wide, enjoying his breaths, as he came into their waiting area. Deputy Morrell was back on the phone with wife Brenda.

“Feel free to do the love note textin',” the Sheriff said as gazes met. “I can't hear it.”

A quiet goodbye to his wife. The phone, still On, was pocketed.

“So, you know,” led Matheson, sniffing into the coffeepot, “I have faith in the elderly. Your grandmother Nance, was military-efficient.”

“Amen, sir.”

Matheson kicked up the reheat on the coffee machine, looked at the filter.

He asked, “Did you see the cylinder was left eye?”

“Yessir,” said Morrell, uncomfortable.

“She explain that one?”

“Yessir. I can't see no one in the world, wanting that.”

Instructional, turning back. “One way we got lost in this nation, is when we stopped being allowed to say 'crazy' was crazy. I knew Kinde at least, a long time. If someone drowned you in *mean* all your days, Lucian, if all was hate and hurt, harm and cruel... you'd want that. The Left Eye, what it would mean. Anyone in the world.”

“But no one went out of their way to hurt either of those vagrants, Sheriff! This one and that one, but not all their lives."

Matheson said, "And you 'just know' that, why?"

From his hip pocket, Morrell's cell phone piped. As if to hide it, he placed a hand atop the spot in his trousers. He sighed as the Sheriff looked at him, as if high-carded again. Trumped.

"Because I'm not crazy."

Nod.

"An abused child cries and cries," intoned his superior. "It wants hope. It wants to know what's happening isn't what life or love, is. And there's a day the child is convinced, as no other explanation's possible. Those eyes, change. Everything gets messed up, then. Like some cult member. Crime is evil, but by me, I call that crazy. Makin' a monster. Both creator and creation, got only their reason."

Presently, hot coffee. Though he had faith in the twin failsafes overseeing the holding room, Morrell fidgeted. He knew anyway, they were on a stopwatch.

No mist or fog, no sheen of either. No haze. The air was clear. What god-spirit, its power as defense or attack, lived under the ground of stone.

The valley was no longer slanted, no hills, no incline. The mineral green, spreading chutes and trunks but mocks of forest, presented perfect symmetry; underneath, endlessly working spirit, had reset them. The valley, all lands stood upright, a flat plane tipped on its side. Unflawed in alignment. Each false, stone "tree", dead living, was in like with another. The battery's array, could be improved no further.

At random, along and throughout this too-perfect vertical evolution, threaded a scrambling object, wild. It was white, the object, and volatile. It stayed within the maze of hard forest, in shudder and quake. It moved without pattern, erratic. It was independent life defined by location. It had no reason, was without Self. It was vermin.

The plain, unreal in exactitude, with only the ever moving stain aside, faced without shield, Before. There was no portal to be seen, but the portal itself was Before. The feminine as energy evolving the masculine land, knew in tandem, where it was. Escape, had been all desired, but escape as passed aeons, tasked cowardly. Neither one force or the other, wished in any sense, to return. War, Justice, inner righteousness, were beauty. Before, was but ugliness. Neither greatness, both things despised in that far place, would touch it. A personal physicality permeated by same, Earth, sickened. They could never be near it, again.

Hence, the white creature of vermin, undulating, careening about the symmetrical stone green. As creation, it was madness and disease. As creation, it would soon be more. The stone array was poised, would be, until that day.

Slowly, Matheson drawing the gurney, Deputy Morrell as anchorman pushing, the twain dead wrapped loosely were out of the deep freeze, back into the main area. There was no room secluded, to move to.

Old doorways narrow and short, left over in the town's departmental building, hemmed them to the one larger space. Ostensibly for receiving cadavers or other, run of the mill deliveries, it was open. A bit warmer than the freezer or outside, but by little. The troopers positioned their charge so to offer themselves free movement.

The rubber mat, too thick to be serviceable, was hauled off and down, draping one side of the gurney. Any excess on the cylinder-side, was pressed, flattened by hand, presenting clear access.

The suicide-murderers, dead and gone, stiff enough, blue-grey, were not so frozen. Clear to any unenlightened what they were, the pair had nonetheless been thawing by decimal points, hundredths accelerated to tenths. The coroner's freezer, after only an hour, had shown poor substitute for Nature. Deputy Morrell said this out loud.

Matheson nodded, but answered, “Me, I'd like to believe if we hadn't found them, they'd both've stayed Chilly Willies, but the heat up's not just Mother Nature wears the title belt. It's inside, their wherever, effectin' this. Look...”

Chin-nod, at the cylinder. There were now definite pinpoints, needle-sized vents dotting wafer-thin casing. Inside, a much thinner cylinder, electric hot pink to bloodred wine, falling, rising. A kind of icicle, the diameter of their pupils.

Morrell admitted, “She didn't get into stages of it. I don't know any flow chart.”

“'Like anything going in to work each day,” said the

sheriff. "You suss based on the moment's evidence, even when you don't know shit for solid. My granddaughter could tell you there's no field a' gilly flowers involved, here."

The deputy squatted, balanced, not touching the gurney. Not about to "yes man" each exchange, he had no comeback. The eyes weren't just in harmony or communication...direct exchange, was in action. Why just now, when it had been perhaps tens of millions of years in their corner of space?

"Their whole thing depends on this connection," he said plain, head shrug.

"Right. It's the idea behind any cylinder, good or bad," said the Sheriff. "If a proper one, we could have another cup, let thaw, feel sorry..."

"Seems you just have to break the connection." Morrell looked up.

Sheriff Matheson's eyes were sad, which offset the sarcastic energy in his reply.

"Interrupt the eye beam, why, genius, Lucian! Watch fingers, I won't stick the Department with a Disability claim, but whyn't you get out your Mastercard, slide it in to block?"

Eyes rolling to spy the too-perfect, too-bright cylinder. Slowly looking straight at it.

Lucian Morrell said, "Magic to me, was always fright stuff, but it always was people right here, doing harm right here. Outer space, sheriff, aeons, evolution...a pressure cooker place? Gazillion years, some revenge meth lab?"

"No shit. 'That look like a special effect to you?"

The deputy, rising, backed away a giant step. Hands up, limp at the explosive riddle.

"They're somehow losing cold too fast. The cylinder can't be blocked..."

"Not if you brought me a steel hubcap," affirmed Matheson.

"Sir, if this is exams, I failed, dock my pay," said the deputy. "Demerit, black mark, bad review..."

"You would have blurted, already," said Matheson, calm and slightly sarcastic. "You like helpin' almost too much. Don't worry about it. What we don't know, we don't."

He bent at the waist, and Morrell backed another pace, tilting head, craning a side-peek. The dead bodies, lifeless but for the cylinder, were motionless. Their faces were horrid, set in what seemed determination.

No, the men didn't know what they didn't. Only what the payout would be, when these hosts soon gave it up.

It had become a reality of seethe. All which could exist Here, ever created or been, was bursting. Yearning to move, move on. Out, to make use of Before, of life not as Here. That which abominated, as through violence it created the gods in blackness, Here. Saved from the destroyers only through escape. Everything since, from mist and rain, rock, grasses to grid, every spark and growth of disease. Its burgeoning, multiplication, extension into all form. There existed no longer any living thing but plague, sickness, disease, highly intelligent contagion, complexities rotating, still finding mutation. Still gaining. Growing stronger, replicating more. In space without dimension, the yearning of purpose gave further feel of density. Constraint. The ready weapon of tales olden, swelled great, chains tearing, danger zones past and ignored. A war-thing, as to at last be fired, freed, unleashed. Set upon. Poison, toxin, sickness, illness, ravaging melt to eat thin paper of human life. Going to Human as spat, a fair test. As the trial of a witch, any flesh being innocent, had naught to fear. Thick, white acid of water and sky, corrosive rivulets, blankets of a sentience, smothering...boiling ...those without guilt, stood resistant. A fact of life in every plane: *Only those Guilty and so righteously judged, died.*

Suffusing the legions of white vermin in union, electric, were two minds one, forever. These gods, long merged, were divine mind animating sick, viscous white. Despite all which had germinated, then bloomed terrible to serve, there was in this un-propertied galaxy outside, only two become one, and what hate...what its holy revenge, created. Comeuppance, have locked itself away for what monstrous Human, Before, would comprehend as “time since the dinosaurs”, yet as Time called “days”. Purpose was forcing the portal, to bathe all human things. Contamination by definition had plenty to go 'round. Only that unloving, cruel, the villainous need fear. Cold, hating demons. The incurably ill, who harmed. Healthy creations, didn't get sick.

Of course, there were no healthy creations. There was no category of rightness. Zero sum, also did not tolerate stasis. Red sun glowing in final days before expiation, illuminated the flaw of very existent form.

With the increasing evidence of thaw as the troopers, empty, struggled at solutions, the dead couple began as unpleasant company, but the lawmen didn't have time to become concerned about that danger. The cylinder in stages, became less disturbing surreal art and began openly functional. Seeming to grind internal "gears". Quickly beginning industrial, unseen motor of sorts, guttural audio. Cylinder hardening to the look of a tarnished golden pipe from eyeball to eyeball, covering both orbs. Faces speaking of animate life, or simulating it. Alarms to the vagrants, their dimension--leaning close twice, brought Matheson and Morrell shrill cries from the bodies, machine system and wounded child in nature. This succession of features in the devolving situation, had Deputy Morrell quaking. Sheriff Matheson just stood there, at one point with arms crossed, hand at his chin. Working on a brain teaser-time bomb, with nothing concrete and no cards in the pocket.

The speed and the power of the harsh gears, increased.

"There's nothing we can do, there's nothing we can do!" Morrell called out, loud. Desperate look to the steps. No exit possible, as he knew enough. Them, Brenda, everyone. The End. Good Night.

"There isn't a solution! Sheriff!"

Matheson, concentration as if a felon held a pistol aimed, grimaced at the dead.

"Bull*shit*, there's nothin' else," he said to himself, then aside to Morrell, "We got one maneuver. It works or it don't."

A wild look greeted him.

"What, say it!"

Matheson pointed, directing.

"Grab hold of that end, brace foot to casters. On '3', twist and tip. We're dumping 'em over, then jump back."

Shocked. "*What?!*"

Menacing, the old sheriff, tall, lurched at the terrified junior.

"Morrell, did you love your Gramma?"

"Well, yessir..."

"Was she a bad woman, a liar?"

More honorable. "No, sir, she never told a lie."

"Then, in 10 minutes or 2, we're dead, maybe the town, maybe the planet, that's right?"

The young deputy glanced at the bodies with their sound and machine-gaze.

"It's poisons, white sick, I know that. A river, she said!"

Matheson spoke faster.

"You know how to stand here and stop 'em?"

"No, sir. Give in."

"Me, either, Lucian. This is 9/11, and phones are for the wall. Grab 'hold and heave-ho!"

Lucian Morrell barked agreement, fearing, trembling, to the far end instantly. Matheson in position, bracing, got his foot in to interrupt movement, and ordered,

"Let me turn half a foot to the wall, then on 3, high tip, throw it ahead and retreat."

A panicked nod. Morrell's face was red and sweat. Almost as straining.

They positioned the gurney. The corpse alert again sounded, more shrill. They were sussed. Matheson grunted as grinding sounds gained speed, and counted. At three, forward. A final half-look showed the cylinder hot yellow, sparks spinning out. Pia's mouth, unlike ever before, was snarling.

The alert from the dead as gods and weapon shrieked as the gurney went down, away from the troopers, bodies barely preceding. Matheson flew at Morrell as the young man tripped, running in reverse.

"Get behind me!" he yelled, but it took two movements. Lucian Morrell cowered behind the sheriff, bastion of the County from his boyhood. Matheson cursed at the gurney-wall and the filth it shielded, .38 drawn, free hand back at the deputy.

In the commotion, there had been a small, smart "snap", as a thick twig of dense wood, and two "pop"s as loud as any Christmas party favor...in the first second of their silence, though both men gasped, there came soft free pouring of fluid. Dead soda, small tipped jugs. Nothing from the aether. No ghostly emissions, no word-sounds. No explosions, no fire. Nothing acidic or nauseating smells, past what the corpses already betrayed. No burning, nothing melting. Short, shallow, dead pouring. It stopped after long seconds. No traces coming around the gurney. They waited minutes. No further sound. The deputy, much younger, thought perhaps he caught the soft purr of more liquid but put a hand over his mouth and drove the thought from his mind. Matheson helped him up. With a hand each to the other's sleeve, the troopers shuffled, slow, hesitant, to peep in stages past battlement of the gurney.

Pia Roeffel and Chelmsford Kinde, their half-thawed shells, lay apart from one another, not touching in any way. Kinde was on his left side, his face partially obscured, but Pia lay 90% on her back, and no mystery remained, either way. Though as they had fallen, the murder instruments, the knives had torn loose, away, nothing to make any state policeman blink. The left eyes of either, Kinde's unseen, were something more than the criminal.

What beyond all understanding was raging oceans in a pressure cooker of years past count, intelligent contagion, multiplicative toxin as collective army, was here, scant ounces of discharge. The cylinder as portal, broken *en toto* before the key moment, did not "work". It held no back up, substitute, no Plan B. No partial or reduced legions. No weaker, diluted waves of plague. The tortured homeless in agreement, had never expected to be found in their secluded, natural scene. The cylinder, minus any freak occurrence, would have held until it didn't hold anymore, Mankind the helpless victim. But that eventuality and simple jostling, if throwback and rough, erased any chance and the anguished torment creating it. No thick white endless verminous liquid. Only more than a half pint each, and of simple pus. White as visible, turned fast to ghastly yellow, as they watched. Lucian ducked down on their side of the gurney, and vomited.

"Don't suppose I ever told you the one from '92," said his boss, still pretending to study the grotesque couple but wryly staring into space. "That young wife in McClellan, town buses crash head on, got thrown through the windshields to one on braking slam, pounded right back in, on collision?"

Morrell heaved harder.

"They say her husband still keeps a black spirit-thing upstairs at home, supposed to be her," Matheson went on. "Kind of a 'hate creature'? But, that part idn't gross."

Their eyes met. The sheriff spoke to the junior officer's apparent anger.

"You pardon the prep, we got clean up before we go home. You won't chuck again, now. And many hands make light work."

Palms raised limp, in surrender. Heck with gross, thought Lucian. He recalled enough from Gramma Nance. Better the barfing. They'd saved the world!

He said as much standing up on his own, turning back on the horrific.

"There's a million-zillion ways it can end," answered the Sheriff, not about to be impressed. "We're one story in the Naked City, Lucian."

As their breathing normed, Sheriff Matheson said, "Welding gloves, and a pair for me. They're in the locker room. And a spare gurney. In awhile, you mix the Spic and Span, *strong*. I'll mop."

Deputy Morrell began to offer thanks, but faltered at chirp-hum of vibration from his pocket.

Scowl. Sharply, "Lucian, by God, does your gal have a life? Give her a child, she needs to keep busy!"

The sheriff left for the locker room himself, an askance composed of daggers, at exit.

ABOUT VOLUME THREE

Even given the unreal "lollipop" tree in the yard, the house wasn't anything unusual. Too-perfectly painted, white. Stock picket fence. Owners Guy and Lorna Teague weren't unusual, either, if coming across as 1950's "suggestions" of people (style of dress, too "I Like Ike", etc). Living quietly in immoral, amoral animal degradation, but as Victorians would. Behind closed doors. Sinners and users and takers. Criminals too, accepted unconditionally by insiders, never tipping their hand with others. The greatest, dirtiest fakes in the world. They'd pulled off their act, shielding death-defying, toe-curling, howling hedonism, for 21 years. That'd be 21 x 2 million. Deception, wore on anyone. It was, however, that time, and the 38 year olds were about to get younger, once more.

The woman's eyes, seeing Ever, Allness set on Repeat, watched out the small window above the kitchen sink. Absorbed in the tree, tall adult but surreal. A silly, couldn't-be tree which didn't grow, sitting placid, "I am here". As were they. One had to accept, to kneel. Give oneself over. Dive in to mortal choice. A tough act, when mortals lived broken immortality. For her, screams of surrender in full embrace, were novocaine. They wore off.

Lorna looked through the perfect square panes set in the perfectly painted window, at the lollipop tree.

Nature's, but as a child would draw. Something conceived via innocence, perceived by any elder as primitive.

"This is as far as it goes," she said needlessly. "17 to 22, 22 to 38, 38 to 50, 50 to 60, 60 to Death Us Do Part."

"Assuming there's a 'death us do part'," said Guy, again playing with her mind. He was leaned into the door jamb. Arms crossed, casual. Manner, amused. The man even walked in a saunter.

Hot menace in her voice.

"Then why do the volumes exist?"

As a litany:

"They were created and bound to hold us to something. Something impossible, in the future of our lives. The set of 5 tomes was pulled whole, from aether, by powers Christians are forbade. They exist, to prevent divorce. We never believed in it, our families didn't. Our churches, certainly not. But shit happens. Therefore, the general history of our life together, set into 5 books. Bound, to bind us."

Lorna was grinning at the yard, the dumb tree, all lack of flaws. Grinning like someone advancing with a knife.

"Like you never thought of leaving."

"I don't obsess, Lornie. We keep none of our vows, screw whomever we wish. Physically harm one another. Worse. We're feral beasts, not people. It's what makes 'us' good. We stay together, because whatever betrayal and pain we deal, we know we're *bound*...together."

"'Til death us do part," said Lorna, turning,

murderer's grin gone but face hard with glare.

"...which can never happen, if the story never ends," said Guy. "Do we have to go over that part?"

He pushed off the jamb, dropping arms. Still instructing.

"In two days, we'll hit the end of Volume 2. Again. Our story has no place to go. For whatever reason, instead of freezing in stasis or ending, we reset. 17, both of us. That first time, on the beach. So happy we're teenagers and the world got simpler, and no matter wh..."

"I get it, 'there's world enough'! *Time!* I got it all the first million years, Guy! I'll be fine in two days! Everything I want! Using everyone! The happiest evil sprite, laughing! *Sinister.* I won't care. I just get like this, when the reset's coming. I understand how trapped we are."

21 years of a finite bond, lived for over forty-two million. Guy Teague, was fine; this was Heaven, to him. To Lorna, close, except those final few months each spin...because she knew he'd hidden Volume 3. Lorna Teague, was shallow enough. She wanted nothing to do with age or death or ugliness, but after the span of an epoch, she wanted to know 'next'. Curiosity. What was coming, aside from no divorce court? Their eternal 21 years ever more decadent, monstrous, edgier. Gibbering simians, shrieking imps. She hadn't had a clean, decent thought for at least ten of those millions.

Punctuating the end, as usual they hosted a housewide orgy, the full day and night before reset. The home was a sea of bodies. Bacchanalia, unbridled. Boundaries pushed until none remained. Lorna made certain Guy was extra drunk, twice as high as usual. Any he used, kept wandering off, disappearing. He saw Lorna from time to time, blood spilling from her mouth. *Really? Pretty out there.* Guy wasn't sure. Only that he had what he wanted. In spades, times ten. Many hours into the sex marathon, he passed out.

He awoke adrift in fine French silk sheets. In their master bed, one never sullied by group play. His brain felt short-circuited; his body, heavy and numb. Guy sank a number of times, dozing, until he recalled he shouldn't be 'here'. The sheets should be NFL in nature, posters of cover girls on the walls. Bleary, he stared at his body, patted his face. Though the man loved himself, he was still on course for age 39.

“Rise, thou chiefest of ten thousands! The chains of pretense, beg be shed!”

She stood in the doorway. Lorna was playing pretend, something at which she was bad. One thing missing from their sex life, was role play, as Lorna blew chunks at it. And this act, was no turn on. Stand up comedy, maybe.

Clad as Cold War space alien. Or robot. Or something. Skullcap of silver, jacket, leggings. Boots. Peaches and cream flesh bazooka-shot with metallic glitter. Eyes, manic as could be affected. Body language, ditto. Vision clearing, Guy could recognize auto spray paint, smell it. The hasty costume was ridiculous.

“Arise, I say!” she as town crier went on. “The time of

Now, is now!"

Guy gaped. Mocking and delighted. To him, the same thing.

"Who are you pretending to be?"

Halting, stumbling through bad lines in a bad play.

"I have shed my pretense as...'sit is time, The Time! The Loyalists have re...resumed theirrr auth-ority, and your place is to...your rightful place, awaits us. We are again Twain Leader."

Guy hesitated, then laughed, goatish.

"Do-*whuuut?!*"

"I do not jest, we return homeworld soon," said 50's space-y Lorna, fists moving from hips to gesture, grandiose, as display model. "The Change has been effect, in...has been effected, and we move forward within it! Go read from the plans of The Master as constructuh...ed. Read from the 3rd tome!"

Trigger. At once, any glee at the confusion, evaporated. Paling visibly, Guy vaulted up, running for their tasteful, carpeted basement. Where sat bookshelves, wall inset, almost as altar. A display of four volumes, gapped.

He almost fell, headlong. Taking the stairs as in a steeplechase. The lights were already on, as Lorna had left them.

The 5 books, in odd appearance, sat completed, on their altar-shelf. Kind of.

The very middle book, was not of the set pulled whole from burning earth. The balancing tome in this arrangement, was taller, far thinner, nothing like those before it or after. It was a child's project of grey construction paper, bound through crafting, with a single pink strand of yarn. Guy saw as he pulled it free, that upon the back, was a dated, silvery sticker of a unicorn. Upon the front, large, in the school-girly hand Lorna's printed text always appeared, "Volume 3: 38 through 50. (Interlude)"

He could hear her footfalls as he opened the pamphlet-thick work, staring at wide margins and bright, neat crayon printing. Labored over. Done with purpose.

"As the end of Youth as agreed neared, the scales fell as one from their minds. As Greaters, discarding useless pretense. Lindar, was calling, though the link had not yet been made. They would discuss, knowing more and more, as they walked. As they walked..."

"Oh, God, this sucks," he said, groaning. Sitting meekly. "Even the way it sucks, sucks."

Silver space alien Lorna, turned from the foot of the stairs. Homemade cap removed, showing wool lining stained from spray. There was silver residue in her permed locks. He saw sparkles come loose as she scratched her cheeks.

"I had to move on," she said, remaining a distance. "I wrote my own. It doesn't match, so what."

"Our life came from primal depths, through ritual," he said, breathing the words, broad stage whisper.

"So did this," said Lorna. "You might not want to use the laundry area, or the bathroom down here, *or* the storage area, 'til I finish cleaning. It's gonna smell for awhile. But I'm on it."

He opened his mouth. She waved him silent.

"Don't. You don't wanta know."

Guy held up the handwritten essay-length effort, showing off the childish construction paper cover. Pink yarn. Unicorn sticker. In growing shock.

"Lorna! Twelve years of 'we're from Gobbledeegook Planet, waitin' for the mothership'? Undercover, or we flaunt it, or...*that's it?!*"

"I don't want all the pleasures anymore, Guy," she said, collapsing down to floor. Looking around at middle class opulence, as one would an empty room. People, their feelings, their hearts, lives...blood...these things mean nothing, they're WTF. I made up a stupid thing about us as stupid, and while you slept last night, got it sanctioned. By whatever whatevers sanctioned Christian teens to be what we became."

Curiosity, "tomorrow" didn't matter, to Guy Teague. Life was no journey, but a buffet. And like most men, his selections seldom varied. He stared at her, adversarial now.

"This is cheating, Lorna."

"Yep. It was my turn."

"You ruined everything!"

"Depends how you look at it. I'm part of this thing, too."

Voice rising, playing The Man.

"If you think I'm going to take this..."

Her own voice cut right through.

"You had your way, stud. For forever. Now, I get to

win. *Enough!*'

Hand, arm stiff, palm down. Motion as stiff, back and forth. Head back, eyes shut. Royalty, dismissing, childish. Guy Teague could only stare, knowing he was going to grow old.

Much later, he slept, deepest rem. Snored, stevedore. "Bastard deserves every nightmare," thought his wife. Lorna, quiet, serene in felt freedom, wandered their home.

The place, even dim, was cluttered. As though who they really were, lived here. The lollipop tree, was now a Japanese maple. Picket fence, actually peeling. This, made her happiest. Lorna would paint it fuchsia.

Downstairs, her righting through wrongs, now nauseated. Damnable odors, raging into olfactories. Lorna felt sick, but not sorry.

She stepped just inside each room stinking loud with sacrifice, glancing at the unspeakable and associated juices. The tasteful basement, a better abattoir. Lorna debated not cleaning at all. Hoping for illness to save her fully. But, that must wait for after 60, still a long way to go. Life as formatted, would continue. Her victory, a girlish thing of craft approved, meant they as couple could move ahead. Not nearly so "overstimulated".

Lorna began up the stairs, but in glancing, found herself reversing to the TV area. Turning on all lights, looking in stark mania to the shelves. High caterwauls as she then searched, tearing up the room, ripping things apart. Hands at some point, bloody. Voice in shriek until past exhaustion. On knees, bruised fists punching air before the altar-shelf of volumes of their sanctified marital bond—with the new #3, childish rewrite, already leaning tired, and the final two, missing.

The Payback Bitch

The Old Ways, including a personal approach, were long evaporated from corporate relations. That world, perhaps not faceless, was now but a suggestion of business, when it came to persons among others. Francois Edgers, couldn't get next to that. The chief executive officer of Cannon Baseline met face to face with people, and he talked with people. He did his own running, kneejerk things, the no-brainers. He was known to be found in the copy room, at HQ, changing out the toner.

He was also known to "pre-hire" assistance, cutting a one-time, small chunk payment as lure to gain favors of experts from areas not overlapping. Stubborn purists, generally committed to "only ____". Between an initial boost for a single work stage and personal contact giving them voice, Edgers moved faster than all competitors, both back in Quebec and on the US' West Coast. He'd said he didn't need a cattle call; he needed those with gifts.

Edgers greeted the attorney pre-hired, who'd barely had time to settle into his lobby seat. The man, Herbert G. Silverman, former assistant DA of Mendocino County, had been early. To both, time was time, and Edgers knew he was immediately appreciated.

"I sent your receptionist to Audio-Visual with some

footage, if you'd like to lower a screen," Silverman said.

They entered the double-sized office, Edgers shutting the heavy door.

"I admire your preparedness," commented Edgers, turning to his desk, where was secreted the control panel.

The attorney seated himself without formality.

"Defenders, nowadays more, just play it Sarah Bernhardt, and make you cry," he said. "I watched one call all nine of our witnesses, 'racist', just before each dismissal. Myself, I never took Theater, in school. For me, it's the heavy lifting."

Herb Silverman, legendary north of Los Angeles, was a smaller man. Correct of manner, shooting from the lip. Spectacle frames for every occasion, and each suit making a statement. Stopping you. Today, the rich pearl grey of "a definite maybe".

"Knowing what Baseline is up against, might mean backing," said Edgers, as the bar area behind his desk, reminiscent of dear camp TV in Herb's childhood, rose and dropped, revealing an oblong flatscreen.

Edgers added, "I'll ask in opening, are we knowingly dealing with infective disease? Poisonous germ cultures? Because, between the cost of elimination and snotty press, our purchase won't be attractive enough. No offense offered, Mr. Silverman, but, it's Fabron Isles."

Say no more," answered Herb, rueful, a twist about his lips. He threw an arm atop the divan he'd chosen. "I never left there, before college...I remember starting for no reason, alone in my dorm room, yelling, *'What was that?'* The answer was, 'nothing'. 'Nothing', flipped me out."

Edgers nodded, grunting, not quite chuckling.

"You have the trail to this point," he said to the noted criminal attorney. "The entire lot and more beyond, acreage extending to a good long jump from the highway."

"Land, spreadin' out, so far and wide," quipped Herb, as he thought again of 60's TV. The reference was lost, but the CEO nodded.

"At Nixon-prices," he said, almost lovingly. "And, since it's Fabron Isles, of course you look but don't touch...but the surveys tell us, this one's safe as well as clean. Right by the highway. Accessibility."

"Again, though," said the counselor, brushing a knee, affecting as though they shared a joke, "it's Fabron Isles."

Edgers touched a button below desk's outer lip, and moved not to sit, but to stand opposite Silverman, against the far wall. Said wall, was all bookcases. Most spines were for appearance.

Reception and audio-visual service, Cannon Baseline stressed in hiring, "military prompt". The screen came alive with Cold War film aged and flawed, proceeding through technology crawling forward. Silverman set up their problem.

"As a way of trading off the Seattle World's Fair and its needle—a lot of people go way too late to anything noteworthy, or have addictive issues and want to 'recapture'--a southwest amusement concern, Idle and

Wilde, broke ground on 'Inland Isle', our ironically named fun center, 500 yards in from the closest beach rocks, about a week before the Cuban Missile crisis. They opened a few days before April, '63."

A period, cartoon-y map, showing placement of rides, exhibits. Designated paths, to and from. To the lower right, southeast quadrant, the problem at hand.

"Inland Isle, serviced mostly locals. In Fabron Isles, there's floating OCD. We never found it boring. Like kids who went every day after school, to the '64 NY fair, at Flushing Meadows. Parents, older kids, us and our friends, the little tykes as they hit the grades. I was there last time, the day after Oliver North was sworn. Inland Isle, was magical. It made you forget. Lotusland, with Lemon Shakeups."

Focus shifted to the workings of the remaining blight in the Baseline's tempting buy.

"'Isles' Island'...the pitchers for I & W thought they were a laugh a minute...was a walking 'ride' of jungle safari, so many let in every quarter hour. You had to remain in groups, not much trouble, there, but a cap, a dime store pith helmet, was originally required, or you couldn't get in. Available at the ticket booth, 30 cents more at first. Some dyspeptic kid got his parents to bring suit, in '72. Settled out of court."

Flat metal suggestions of snarling animals, not repro photographs but overdone painted images, popping up from behind plastic brush; ditto zoo cages constructed as in full decay. Animal flats would rotate into sudden view, past the bent 'bars'. A larger beast, biped, jamming paw at the perfect angle, through illusory 'damage'. A python, as crooked spear, doing the same. Silverman was tense, watching; Edgers, who treasured postwar American kitsch, was in this minute, at ease.

Silverman: “Early sound sensitive tech, was employed. The wrong movement, loud enough, or tonal quality, inflection, could summon 'attacking animals'. Another, might make some or all, vamoose. Dismiss one, buy the appearance of two others. Vice versa. Jungle beast buddies after your happy band, in the form of shock. Tiny cork rifles, were originally supplied to groups; the alphas loved them. Dyspeptic kid. '72. Court. Home of the brave.

“Inland Isle, like any happy fun ha-ha and hot dog place, had its tragedies. A total of 5 deaths, the last, in 1980. They coped by the nanny-route, and hired more people as guides, who instead acted as scolds. The loyal never stopped coming in, but interference always scares people away, and by '84, losses spiked. The town wanted it, there was a letters campaign, a sit in...I & W took it on the chin for longer than they should have.”

A suited man, making some pacifying speech. A sea of sad faces. Little kids with shop-processed placards: “They Took My Dreams Away”. A bulldozer colliding with a sorcerer in turban. A Buck Rogersesque spaceship, crashing to the ground.

“The place closed, in 1989,” said Herb. “Unlike the rest of the layout, no demolition to Isles' Island, they just left it. Management claimed they would only erect and doubly reinforce fences. They did, and adventuring looters played their game. Until '95, when Idle and Wilde updated to electrified fences topped with razor wire, ten people were reported lost on the property. 'Near it'. 'In vicinity of'. Local government, the usual false redirects. This was during Rex Cromwell's *reign*, I can call it that."

The CEO, was bending, slightly. Trying not to laugh aloud. Herb was not one to refrain from leveling up.

"You're certain you want this land?" he asked, shifting, as the screen began into the real problem.

"*He's* not in charge, anymore," said Edgers, matter-of-fact. "He just never goes away. You have to deal with him."

"I got that," said Herb, absently checking the sole of a shoe.

Security camera footage, sequences longer to brief. None of it sharp; cameras brought hard about due to motion, to spy air. A tip of something. A curve of something. A digit, or disappearing profile. A small, hovering baby's back, wingspan wide, from it.

Silverman watched Edgers, who stepped forward. The clips, from days of Desert Storm into 10 years of the Millennium, were many. Most, could be your vision, no matter how often you thought you were certain. More than half a dozen, including a laughing peek through leaves, would give no jury time for their free lunch. The attorney, already familiar with particulars of this local stain, seemed even faster than he was. Knitting the visual story of Isles' Island together for Edgers, was almost rote. Herb'd had time for Porterhouse, the

Mariners-Orioles doubleheader, and the weekend had still been boring.

The CEO, once the flatscreen presented a menu then went dark, turned. Without expression. Counselor Silverman nodded. “Yeah,” he said. Francois Edgers, as if a smoking gun needed clarification, asked,

“Do we have any HD or better-footage?”

Silverman pecked the air, crooked finger.

“That's all, Loch Ness as it is,” he said. “Updates were due, mandated, paid off and ignored, even after Y2K. All cameras and mechanisms pulled, December, 2010. City bought the ride—literature always and forever, has it a 'ride'. And everything around, is chalkdust.”

Chalkdust, was of no concern to corporate interests. Whole horizons of blank, begged filling in. Edgers had brought in the noted criminal prosecutor, for the very reason a driver stuck for better problem knowledge, hit the gas. Silverman, noted for shunning corporate law, had greeted with completed upfront work, transitioning fast to problem's reactor core.

“So,” Edgers said, “what are those grainy images, supposed to be?”

Herb Silverman, devoid now of smiles, spoke to Edgers, then spoke to the screen.

“Any dark leather...spiny, nail-like wings? That's a—not kidding--transformed survivor, from an idiot looting. That smaller, the pink-whitish, vaguely baby-thing, is the original problem. It made the other, into what we see...what little I could link, assuming agreement, is in a compiled dossier. As for the little creature, I've spoken with survivors, already. None I could assess, ever knew the others, but oddly, they all give the same branding.

"They call it The Payback Bitch. Apparently, it does."

Without decorum, Francois Edgers cut it short. Silverman was valuable beyond hopes. Truthful honesty, was gold. You didn't waste that.

Simply, "Options?"

"*Carte blanche*, or back," said the attorney. "If action, I know who, what's needed...but, *it will not be easy*, and mess will occur. I'll handle that, too. If 'no', I'll say it's been awfully nice, meeting you, sir."

There was no calculating, how much Cannon Baseline held in assets. Edgers, last year, had listed in the Top Ten Richest Citizens of Quebec. He didn't know Counselor Herbert Silverman, only *of* him, and a notebook of urban legends. By all standards, the extended lot was being given away.

After only a short pause, Edgers bowed his head, saying into his collar, *sotto voce*, "You know of the van der Weyden rendering, 'St. George and the Dragon'?"

Herb Silverman was silent, waiting for inevitable eye contact. He then said to Edgers, in that same stage whisper, "Yes. I hear the one hanging at London's National Gallery, isn't the original."

And neither could quench their grin.

The men, a standard squad, were professionals. A number had worked together, before. Three, had fought overseas, real actions. Only one, had done time. There was a sometimes "camou dude" from Area 51; his deeper resume, checked out. The beefiest, wielded an old rocket launcher, vintage cherry Falconet. They were paid; a promise of double, to any two who made kill. None were from Fabron Isles, but every one, believers. This safari, was realized dream. As a group, they figured to lose two or three. None of these, naturally, would ever be themselves.

It was ten minutes-plus before dusk, as almanacs said; they therefore had fifteen of truly good light, ten more, of "okay". There were night goggles already on. No jokes existed, among them, and Herb Silverman didn't crack any. Privately, Herb didn't think they'd be allowed in, not deeply. Their point guard of three, had just fixed bayonets.

As he was handed his personal choice, a Smith and Atchisson "Punch Gun"--a pistol shotgun loaded with trademarked, "no-scatter" acidic shells--Silverman chanced to stare right, toward the Interstate, football fields' away. Cycle cops had diverted off-road, on their side, and what foolishness followed them, had filth out of Silverman's mouth the mercenaries found impressive. Eyebrows raised, and a pair of men high-fived.

Silverman stopped, hung back as he noticed the vehicles slide from the frontage road. The security team questioned from behind, but the Counselor bade them be silent, knocking a hand backward. Herb's face was fast to the sardonic, at what was coming. Walking with a slow 360 in his gait, Silverman pacified the guards, indicating they were to wait.

Then, he was removing gloves, on course to intercept incoming parties, trying to put more than discreet distance between Isles' Island. At point of exact identification, he stopped, feet apart. Smiling, unfriendly.

A matched pair of California Highway Patrolmen astride cycles, helmeted, in full uniform. They had to be off the clock. To their rear, a blued metal-in-gloss, custom late model Chrysler PT Cruiser, always very Capone, very Bugsy. Where hood ornaments traditionally sat, a desktop California State flag...but the old, "supposed" one of speculation, with the two antiquated shades--one greenish, one a yellowed orange, disallowed from the spectrum--and angry Poseidon stretching forth his hand. So pretentious. The asshole only employed this, if his mood was good.

The CHP's slowed, stopping perpendicular from Silverman, who felt hot wind hit his legs. The chalk of the ground, made for endless expanse. Like it was one of those clandestine meetings on only-so-tough television, the "gun" question hovering in the air.

"You stopped way too soon," he greeted long-ex-Mayor Cromwell, as Rex swiveled out, to concrete.

Herb pecked a crooked finger, high. South.

"Evita's way down that way."

"'Never required to lean, Herbert," said Rex, plastic grin wide, as he approached.

"That's not what I heard."

Rex shrugged.

"Well, then, you heard wrong. Lots of misinformation, these days. Damned Internet."

Cromwell, was near a head taller. Not known as a close stander, he pressed just the right distance in, for effect.

"What are you here for, Rex?" asked Silverman.

Head turned to glimpse the fence, the men. Cocked, then, at the attorney.

"Don't go in there, Herb. You don't want to go in there. And they don't either, FYI."

Amusement in Silverman's frown.

"So, it's due to you?"

Cromwell did a better judgmental expression.

"I'm not serving *you* confession! Today's special, is blood-soaked guts."

"Thanks, I'll just have water," said Herb. "I don't do even multiple-party corp buyouts, Rex, not with speed bumps galore, but here I am, as everything must go. That means your sun-roofed vault of Monster, there."

A jerked thumb, back. Rex looked surprised.

"Okay, you fooled me. You've got teeth sunk in. You're good. So, if you've paid them, squeeze it to write-off. Why this? You know, already."

"A monster, you mean?"

Cromwell was close to laughing. Delighting in the legal sharpie he'd dodged throughout the years. The one while in office, Rex had dubbed, "the little man".

"You know, Herbert, no one can seem to remember this, but I once had a kid sister. I was 12 when she was 6. I'm good for a carafe of chianti, I understand you enjoy that, if you'd spare an evening to hear the tale. But, it's the only freakydeak I'm hiding.

"There are beings inside that fence. One's a way-better thing, hard as stone—internally, as well. It kills. It thinks it owns the grounds."

Silverman turned head, catching the far boundary of fencing, in periphery.

"Just why would it think that?"

Rex stepped back and with timing, retreated.

He said, "Right now, the attorney for the Defense is asking the judge if Mr. Cromwell is qualified to comment on ethereal psychology. You elect to withdraw the question, I'm dismissed, and you call your next witness."

Herb shook head, making a face, snapping fingers.

"God, yeah, what order were they in? The next witness, is...uhhh..."

"I don't do requests," said Rex, and before spinning to cruiser, intoned, "Remember how your friend, Teague, died that night? Blood never dies, Herbert. Legwork. Legwork."

Silverman had no comeback. Before slamming the door of his prize chariot, the PT in blue-glaze, Cromwell again said, "Cross their palms, Herb. Send 'em home. You'll get your goons killed. Worse, is possible."

Power long gone, rolled past around right, rejoining the frontage road, further distant. Herb Silverman told those hired there was a warning from sources, and blessed each with one more "C"-note. After security left, he stood in front of the chained entrance. Leaned, eventually, against the ticket booth. Staring past them. Hearing his great friend from high school, shrieking how it hurt. Great Friend's Great Love, in tone of hot tar, calling the staff "cold butchers". Telling all gawkers, how she hated them.

There was a spot dedicated as memorial, inside Isles' Island. "The High Ground". The fence, reared penitentiary-tall, hid it, also. Counselor Silverman would have his answer, if he could just stare for one second, at that spot. He didn't go in. Didn't try. Bought a bottle, on the way home.

Saturday, early. He wasn't looking forward to this. Herb had put it off, dismissed it...after all, it lent speculative truths credibility, shed paranormal light, and if you'd grown up in this town then gone on to a world of hard facts and bottom lines—however unsettling or sick—things unexplained easily explained, became low. Embarrassing. You knew they were real, a bigger bag enveloping realities "everyone" knew, but most were unfriendly, stygian. And still, to outsiders, you were a dribbling space cadet. Herb Silverman knew what inhabited ringed Isles' Island. That one at least, existed as killer, only figured, but if you permitted the thought, it existed therefore as hate beast. One which sought to "take back". But, all things died. Shit happened, and there you were.

By the time he parked in the lot of Darlingwood Nursing Home, Herb had steeled himself. Finding only one accessible space, he allowed a driver's frustration to override old images of terror. He squeezed his Fleetwood Brougham, tucking it as close as possible through backing, into the space just beside the primary curve...then sat, looking, hunted, as three other vehicles passed too-near his door. Next to that, greeting the receptionist, asking directions and his hoof to Room 417, was mindless. Herb took a cleansing breath, before even he pushed open the door.

Two beds in the private room, both made, meticulously. The room itself was long enough, but rather narrow. A tube television dark, dusty. An old style pink radio on the builtin counter area. A few items about. On the wall above said counter, one exactly: hanging above the head of the far bed, a mini font meant for hand dipping of holy water, an antique style mocked as clamshell, madonna behind it, faded. A calendar, old, at the curl, hanging as from it. Herb could not make out the year.

The woman seated between the beds, was barely older than Herb by any measure of Time, but looked a decade older. Darlingwood had an in-residence salon, and she availed herself to perms, but they didn't often employ the best help at these places, and dye laid down last visit permitted stark white threads amongst the gold. Showing nebulous weight gain, her face was much more engorged, as though stung by bees, but without marks. At least dressed for the day, her garb was “thrift store”--sweat shirt, dark blue, had rips at cuff seams. Herb Silverman remembered her in crisp, fine cuts of outfits, kneeling by her work at dedications. In backless ball gown, receiving federal honors. For—was it eight years?--she had been a "name", a real profile, a big footprint. *"The emerging sculptress of our times."* Lorna Jensen, once consort to a departed pal. A sidebar, then cover corner, in *Newsweek.* Worth far more than Silverman, in the 90's. Nursing home fixture. Dowdy. Sallow. Forgotten.

Lorna's face shown upon taking him in. Weak from walking so seldom, the woman flailed as she tried to rise.

"Hey, you," Lorna said, openmouthed with happiness. Despite Herb waving her seated, she'd pushed on to her feet by the time he'd strode to her. Embrace. She felt like warm lead to the lawyer, and for that, weak as the proverbial kitten.

Herb helped Lorna back into her chair. Sat with her. Inquired after her strength (*"Scale. I'm 50something going on corpse."*). Spoke of her brief brilliance (*"I'm a sucker for permanence, Herbie. But nothing is."*). If there remained any left, any family (*"You watch the Olympics, every four, right? 'S how often I get to hug loved ones."*).

There was real hopelessness, here. Herb didn't try and ignore it. The woman who'd once received the Medal of Peace for her "Dove is in Hand", a high, faceted two piece sculpture giving illusion of bird in flight yet held by Creator's Hand, had given up. Not yet 56, Lorna was just an old woman. She sped past, cut through and stopped short on any attempts, but of high school...and of those days, it was Guy, and her and Guy, and that terrific, funny, smart, protective, heroic, godlike Apollo in the sun, Guy Teague. Something locked away which Silverman never allowed out, basked in it, and he willingly gave Lorna the floor, amending no memories.

The accident, was of course recalled. The too-aged matron in the midst of her memories, regardless to Silverman slipped in and out before him, seated sometimes on grasses at dusk, a teen with bloodcoated hands. Eyes, blindly casting around, never to see value, again. "People, don't care," said the girl to his silence. "They kill others. People, are demons in skin suits."

The last thing the attorney wanted, was to broach his own subject. Hurtful as it was listening to Lorna, Herb waited well into "Guy Teague as statue never cast"...then, swallowing as he began, asked what he'd always suspected. Herb could have avoided assembling the soldiers of fortune, he'd known that, but Rex's taunt, bore weight. Cromwell thought him an idiot, anyway, but Herb resembled that remark, when prideful. Like any biased, selfrighteous citizen, he didn't want the sad and suffering to be guilty.

"I'm trying to arrange the sale of the Inland Isle lot," he told her, finally to it. "The entire acreage. The old spooky's stuck to it, shit on designer label. I've called up video, 1990 to days before they took down the cameras. Like you, I don't forget faces. Not one that matters.

"The R.I.P. cherub you chiseled for their High Ground, rules the lot. It's taken a lot of payback, already, Lorna. Did you know this?"

Silverman, had consummate prosecutor's eyes...in a way, gambler's eyes were as steady, as clear to "knowing". Though, one could not ferret The Hand of Fate out of any betting equation; a wager involving play, always contained that gremlin, its "whammy". An attorney on the side of Thou Shalt Not, knew, or enough. He was then doing math. But Lorna didn't try to hide it.

She returned Silverman the dirty gaze of war, and a mouth seeming to eat. The counselor sat, calm, pokerfaced. He'd only heard of 'this' Lorna Jensen, in teenhood, and only from biased, errant sources. Herb had been quick to judge, then. No calculation, involved.

Lorna, empowered: *"Does she still look like me?"*

Herb's heart, cinched. Belly, housing chill. Sickness. She'd let the bad thing destroy it all.

"Anything footage showed," he admitted, "was small scale Lorna Teague. No one else knows what they're looking at."

The senior shuddered visibly at his use of the married tense, one never made legal, only ever a pledge. Herb nodded peace to her.

"It doesn't shock me, it's sentient," he told her. "And, I figured a couple of those missing looters just...did the wrong thing. You don't tempt guards, not police, not Other beings. ...but eleven, have gone missing, and...you know what had to happen."

"Call it the old take on Law, Herbie," she returned, eyes at once belligerent. "That's a burial ground, whether he was laid there or not. Sacred ground, anyway."

There was cold, in the room. He couldn't believe she still felt this way.

He ramped it up.

"She has an *aide de camp*, now, Lorna. One of those young thieves, she somehow 'made' like her. I don't know how; you, possibly do. Ebon, charcoal black. Taller, slight. Her lieutenant..or, her fodder. How does your 'she' have powers as creator?"

"*I* created her, using *my* creative powers," Lorna said. Hard about it, and righteous. "Each made thing, is of a kind. The hand, making, imbues. Soul, heart...longing, aches, these proceed into creations. No poetry to it, though, Herbie. I'm not this used up this early, because of mourning or drink.

"I'm the bitch, kiddo. I birthed her from pink granite, and in private ritual, I gave her Me."

The eldering woman's smile, signo, deep smirk of trump card laid, graced a face with no reason to care.

Calmly, measured, Silverman asked, "Who is this helper-girl? The 'convert'?"

"I didn't know that shit! I don't receive reports. It's like having a child who lives in another land, overseas, the Pole, you're lucky to hear anything! My guardian-Self was created for a purpose, and I get she's still serving it, very well."

"Lorna...it was a stupid, meaningless accident. The flange, the metal python, released on tonal cue."

He'd retreated to prosecutor. Invalidating flawed testimony. But the truth, was too close. They stared at each other.

"*Say it,*" she demanded.

"You blame damned, dumb kids, a couple of 'em younger than *you.* If I'd handed you an Uzi, was that going to bring Guy back for two seconds?"

"You never lived poor, did you, Counselor?"

Patiently: "...and you didn't either, Lorna."

"I lived poor all my life," she said. "I was poor as a millionaire. Watching the world of hand-in-hand."

As though bullied, she continued, "They all stood there, Herbie. Stood there. Cow eyes. I've got my hands to his chest, he's crying out so loud..."

"I remember. Shut up."

"...they all stared, and more at me. Part time trash. Useless flesh. *They didn't care.*"

"Nothing could have helped, Lorna. If the park had an ambulance. He was dead in five minutes! Six!"

"...because the steel trap, the animal picture, slid out," Lorna said, dry of eye. All cried out. "He was goofing, like he did, back to the bars..."

"Shut up, girl. It's on the backs of my eyelids."

Mock of happy surprise.

"My Lord, we must us be related, then! Can you see Guy's face just before? And right after?

Still speaking to him, not seeing him.

"There's not enough justice, Herbie. You should know."

Unacceptable. He at least, had changed.

"Lives taken, young lives?"

"We reach there. We had ours taken, two ways. Guy

died. Good for him."

He knew he was on sacred ground. Herb remembered Guy Teague, remembered the couple. Dawn of the 80's, lighting them all a new world. His friend never got to taste of it. Guy's consort had by choice, tasted then, vinegar. Giving him their child, her own gremlin, to rule a hallowed ground. Whammy, for those who dared not remove their sandals. Tomb with an unknown, in it.

"Lorna," he began, pausing as her gaze became a pit fighter's. This was territorial. And like a bitch itself, this was all she had.

"Our birthplace is five hundred times, shrouded," he reminded her. "Fabron Isles, is far more, than some odd town. There's more dark, more 'not right', here. But people must live, they have to, they will. They're going to. It could be another decade. Maybe long enough, I'll sit in some home like this. But the right money will be wampum spread, and the right deal, illegal as Cuban cigars, struck. And they'll go in, the demo crew, and your guardian will rise up, and everyone's just gonna know..."

"I hope they know!" Lorna yelled, all whine, so torn Herb disconnected, stepping back to Zen of his work.

"Don't act like you share this, Herbert! You had an awful scare, a bad night! Maybe it lingered. Oh, well! How many, have you called 'friend', through the years? You think all loss, is the same? That there's one reaction, and we march over the dead? That works, from a shrink's couch."

Leaning forward. Looking ready to pounce.

She said, "You didn't make any noise. There were all kindsa people present, all yang-yanging away...but in that one second, church-quiet. Except for me."

The "safari" grounds, were all around. The fake zoo, made no sense in such a setting. Guy, born to theater, dancing moron, backing to the bars. Probably, he thought it was safe—two slide-springing animals had already loomed, and behind the bars. That grin on his face. Always happy to be "him". Was the hubris a gag? You always had to laugh. He was tall and fit. He was young and strong. Their world was new. Everything was new.

He was standing to the side, more than a yard away. Arms folded; Herb always got cold, at night. Glancing back, at Lorna. She beamed at Guy. His biggest fan. Only a few, paid attention. Lorna, never looked away.

She hooted, hollered, some Deep South football noise, clear as a police whistle, long burned away from his memory. Herb could never reproduce it. Impossibly, that rare pocket of no talking, no sounds. Everything dropped away as the cheer rang, burst. A judgment.

Guy was square to a breach, bars rent, comic curves. Over the top. And Herb saw his friend Guy Teague as impresario and king of the world...blink...murdered, ended, chest and abdomen of red. Victim of impalement. The head of the python, too fast through to be obscured, was looking at Herbie Silverman. Like the Disney character, years before--the image was too akin, they could have sued. The snake was grinning. It knew.

Her face was, though reasonably without hope, as a judge or ten he'd known, who wanted no more of Counselor Silverman's extraneous bullshit. *You want Justice, little friend? Make him live, and all of us.*

Satan casting out Satan. A hole dug, to remove the first one. And all in.

He tried the raw of it, the end.

"You had life, all life, Lorna. We all did, each of us. You chose this?"

Vision into zealot's glow.

"We each make choices."

Onto his feet, out of the chair. As he moved, sidestepping, Cannon Baseline's legal hire told Lorna Jensen,

"I'll give their CEO the truth, in one big bite. If still he somehow doesn't back, it's world news. The ante will be missiles, or the Dark Ages with cell phones. Everyone has a deep wound, Lorna. Your guardian, gives that right of way."

Courtroom dramatics granted even Herb Silverman only so many seconds. He turned, almost missing her rhetoric.

"Arrest me, Justice. Finish this. I have nothing, and never did."

Silverman replied with meaning, "That's why no charges will ever be filed. You've done life, already. For other, curious citizens, Lorna? Good luck."

True to his word, in a closed, Sunday meeting at

Cannon Baseline, Silverman filled in Edgers all new information. He carefully omitted his connection to Lorna and Guy as a couple, as well as his presence, the night of Guy Teague's death. Detailed also, a story to then unspoken, of Lorna, still stable as could be detected in her salad days as "emerging sculptress", dedicating the light pink granite cherub so very close in visage to her own at 1-5 scale, for what had been negotiated as "The High Ground". Replete with plaque dedicated to Guy Wilson Teague, I & W expressing penitence not pursuable further in court. Herb remembered; he'd been there. The subdued applause, the reverence for this calming, this peace. Lorna, posing next to stone cherub Her. Holding on, embracing, as would a mother.

Of course, Edgers didn't back. The additional info wasn't skewed enough to learn more; they already knew the foe was paranormal. Origin, as it was humanbased, mattered little. Silverman was told to proceed.

Necessary calls were made. The same soldiers of fortune, even the pedigreed camou dude, were rounded up—as he'd chosen them to start, any replacement team wasn't going to be as good, and starting from scratch was a waste of time.

As before. They assembled outside the chained gate. The weapons master handed Herb his shotgun pistol open, allowing him to inspect. He thanked the man but barely paid attention, giving the highway an accusing look. Serendipity could be asshole.

No grand entrance. Rex and his ego never appeared,

and Herb Silverman, default commander by way of American dollars, ordered the chains cut, the gate opened quickly, and for the bayonet men walking point, to advance. *Everyone else, fall in behind, out-curved on the sides. Max attentive, to blind spots.* He himself, would be positioned dead center. Herb deliberately used those words.

Not a dozen yards in, their vaunted formation began to meld, to soften, mix. “Smoosh”. Attention to blind spots became for some, walking backward, covering the rear. The squad-plus-Herb, by the time it veered through the initial area, harkened to special effects lampooning fanatical Secret Service, or editorial cartoons of survivalists. Silverman called out places known to him as housing traps, animal flange, and these were given a wide berth. Though, even the underground batteries for emergency against ocean cold, were dead many years. Traps sprung as what had killed his friend and broken Lorna's mind, were not the enemy, now. Someone snarled at the Falconet's toter, to “keep it elevated!” No one stayed completely quiet. This monster, they could never sneak to.

The green and mottled tones of their group shuffled, a few stepping high, through overgrowth. A lot of the grass was brown. Patches. A few patches of bare ground. Herb watched toward a high trapeze, from which an illusion was known to swoop. The thing, little pinkish monster angelbaby, could not withstand their might, but they needed all or most of it. Surprise, bleeding them, a suddenness would cause them to break. It would be nice to think they were united, but names like The Alamo and Little Big Horn were historic, for a reason.

They wound toward Guy's place of death. Some spat, from nerves; Herb's own mouth, was hollow parch. The Smith and Atchisson, a nickel plate, was wet against his cheek.

Again, calling a danger area. The blob of squad stepped, back and side, from the zoo trap. Herb watched the spot. The snake, python, would never be seen, again. Herb saw Guy, so full of himself. Heard the screams, then the sobs. Lorna, begging every empty face, to help. He got her. Herb understood. But you couldn't do this.

Slight pushing, resistance, loose mutter to "halt". Herb caught cloth in his mouth.

"We have one already down, up The High Ground!" said a point man, calling back.

All three of those guys, wore night goggles. There was light yet, too, plenty, but they had the best specs. Silverman shoved, ordered. Pushed his way to the front.

The High Ground, looked neither high or wide. It was not majestic, of course long untended. The grasses, always cut as golf course green, were bare, mostly, and brown. Its lone palm still stood, slow winding, corkscrew. The bush to the right, was darker than ever, blackgreen--full, but appearing fake. The plaque in the middle with Guy's name and that of this spot, was polished, giving impression it had been a regular chore. The cherub presented free to Fabron Isles, all park patrons, the amusement concern of Idle and Wilde, was not there.

Another angelic-demonic winged being, dusky leather, woman-sized, lay across it. Claret as sparkling, garden party refreshment, spilled from its maw and ran off the plaque. The unearthly beast, in seizure, twitched. It quietly cried. Some, whispering, thought it was dying. All, bunched as in camp horror, approached at a creep. Herb had already put away his Punch Gun, and left them behind. The black thing saw him, and tried to move. It was in deep pain. Herb glanced around, above, and took the several steps up toward the fairly low "high".

"It's okay to kill me, it's okay to kill me," the succubus, ebon leather, spiny of bat's wings, beseeched. In a very human female voice.

"I died a lifetime back," it reasoned, then contorted, as though having taken a slug, unheard. The succubus-bat spoke loud enough, but shining crimson ran out of its mouth and onto the plaque, from the effort.

Herb began close in. It was very hurt. There had been a definite confrontation.

"Did you war?" he asked. "Throw down? You took some chunks out of it...?"

He noted chips and pebbles of granite, bare pink stained with red.

"Please say...?" asked Silverman, squatting, unafraid of the transformed creature. "Did she hit you, your mouth? Did you bite each other?"

Whites of eyes, far back in sockets. The ebon demon moaned, crying, because its laughter brought great pain. Resistance overridden, Herb offered a hand, and the suffering thing squeezed it, with both claws. Not superhuman. Not human, either.

"I ate her," was the confession. A man more to the rear, began to bar laugh, and was smacked by another, threatened by a third. Herb didn't take his attention away.

Blood undried, was like bad lipstick on the thing. It tried to lift its head, and as thin paint, some ran down its chin.

"I got told a few sentences," Silverman said. "The cherub wouldn't have created an equal, in any way."

It laughed itself into great suffering, again (*"Cherub..."*), and a minute went by.

"You're right," the thing said. "Greater, doesn't want equal...just a great other being to sit on."

"Three were killed, one kept to 'become'," Herb recited from findings. "Yours, in 1995, was the last raid. Who are you?"

It looked at its claws, clutching Herb's normal if spotting hands. He knew then, she was dying, and knew she had to.

"I was Cherise Lowe. We were trapped, bunched in a corner; she was going to mow us all down, drench the ground."

"She said this? Could talk?"

"In a person's mind. You would think it was your own mind, but it would make no sense, so you'd know. Think, and know."

He sat next to her. A hand to her neck. The bat,

demon, creation once Cherise, had silver rain on her face. As grateful and with thanks as anything could be. Persons, included.

"Did you ever once, attempt escape?"

Cherise took one claw back, to indicate her face.

"To go where?" she asked.

He was silent.

"Forever with her, me as supplicant," Cherise continued. "I knew the grounds'd one day go. Your abort the other night, had...there's a name for her, a personal one, but I won't chance speaking aloud..."

"Got you," Herb nodded, gently.

Receiving a water canteen, he offered. "Human H20," he joked, apologetic.

Cherise shook her head.

"Water, helps, and life," she said. "I don't want extra seconds."

A beat of reverent silence.

"She was readying defense," Herb said it as statement.

"...and I was the only Other accepted, her's remade, ally. I'd never rebelled, only obeyed, listened. So long... I shouldn't have ever existed as this, but if a being knows...if you stand loyal, ready, *years going by...*

"Quietly," Silverman breathed, and the joy this brought Cherise, made her seizure from agonies. As these subsided,

"Quietly," said Herb, again, "you as lone other and from her touch...*you made her trust you.* Quietly, Time went by and she trusted you."

The immediate internal pain drove back any further

mirth, but Cherise winked in response.

"I was outwardly a new creation, through her. I told her, if as supplicant I took her inside me, it doubled strength, resistance. Everything. An Us. I was her, so nothing harmful could result. A fuel as her spare self, her running it. In charge."

"How could some ascended power, buy that?" asked one of the men, some guy behind Herb.

"All you can do, isn't the same as what you know," Cherise said, more to Herb. "Monsters, can kick your ass, tear down your house, and still be stupid. My words, were gibberish. She bought it, praised me--don't you know, we were one and the same?"

The same man began objection, but Silverman shut him up with, "Brainiacs, can be stupid, too. Powerful shits, are often full of shit."

"I made certain sheez' dead, right off," said ebon, batlike Cherise, beginning toward death, herself. Trembling. "Stone...no screeching. I just broke and bit in vital ways, angles. And that was the end, and she didn't know it. That evil savage, deserved a hundred deaths. You do what works."

The teen girl cursed to this prison, much as Lorna housing only lost things, moaned. Cherise was crying, silver rain. Herb whispered to her, and hummed. A few muscleheads, offered to finish her; Silverman was regarded as bearing the right of command. He shook his head. Again, he held hands with the creature once Cherise Lowe. Told her she was a hero, had saved others. Had mattered. That she was good. Though Herb barely recalled the cadence, toward the end, he said Kaddish. This had long ago been a girl with dreams, like Lorna Jensen, like all had dreamed. Cherise stared at him, never breaking eye contact, until she died. She tried to smile with her bleeding mouth. She took in Herb's every word. She looked at him with love.

He felt her go, managing, "go to sleep". Catching a breath, the attorney saw a number of the mercenaries had removed their caps; several, kept heads bent, in mourning. He found himself staring further into the grounds, to grassy murk. Wondering about a world where Guy had stepped away, in all his jackassery, seconds earlier. Or a reality where they'd ridden to the park, a minute later.

No man hesitated, in bagging the body, lifting teamwork, onto transport. It was to be dealt with by better paid agencies, and swiftly removed. Though some hardcores, rifles at presenting level, looked about with menace, they had no reason to stay. Herb Silverman certainly did not. A devotee and practitioner of the Court System, he trusted instincts as long as they were his. He waited until minutes after the gurney bearing the tragic, selfless woman was out of sight, then himself made a beeline for the gate.

He was fifteen minutes outside boundaries, before he got through. Herb kept walking away, until everyone got the hint. Once connected to the switchboard at Darlingwood, he asked to speak to the head nurse. After a hesitation, Herb was asked to call back, as the RN was in business currently with mortuary assistants. One of the residents had just passed. The attorney said thanks, hung up. He stared at his phone.

Monday, mid-morning. Silverman was due to deliver time-sensitive papers they could not, in this case, be trusted in other hands. Traveling down to Redding, handing off over lunch with Edgers. Running late as it stood.

Smiling at the OCD of it, Herb pulled his Cadillac into the same, open side space as before—this time, by choice. Speaking with no one, he entered Darlingwood, that clean, shining, uplifting place of keeping good attitudes about Death. Retracing steps to the second floor, and to room 417. The door was closed, "NO ENTRY" sticker of yellow and red and black across the doorhandle. He peeled away the sticker and walked in.

They'd cleaned, already. It was antiseptic, as far as he discerned. Dim. He didn't flip on any switches, and observed by sunlight angling through the far window.

No possessions remaining. No trace the debilitated sculptress had ever lived here. But near the far wall, that calendar. Hung from the disused hand dip for holy water. Clamshell, faded madonna at its back. Lorna, had never been that person, to have this. It had belonged by way of a grandmother, to Guy. He had not been that person, either. When they and others had stood together, young, it hit Herb they had not been anyone, yet. Lorna was right about one thing: *choice, was individual.* Like her's. Like Cherise Lowe's. Choices, were terrible things. Things which alone, imprinted the world, and Life. Heartsblood, souls bellowing imprint.

What a goddammed terrible thing.

He stared, never moving closer than midroom, at the bitty-calendar. Even wearing a brand new prescription, Herb could not make out the month or year. Only one thing certain—the first digit, was not a two.

"*God*," the counselor breathed. Hanging head.

Outside, he glanced at his watch. No avoiding it; Herb would be pretty late. He didn't like it, but shit just happened and Time, it marched. Life, man. Nothing, got a single thing back.

WE ARE THE COIN (PT. #2)

The old dude, military of dress, passionate in last words, left the world with head tilted far back. Eyes, the same. Something within, going outward. Guy stared at the fear and ecstasy written on that face. Monolingual, the teen had made out nearly nothing... mostly, the infamous historic name, "Peron".

The teen, naked, out of place inside the time capsule he and his lover had invaded, straightened. Very warm, here. Baking warm. Itching, without itching. The open rooms, were wrecked; the incomprehensible spaceship-bell had fallen sideways, on landing.

Rattling, clanks, breakable objects falling. Guy turned, balancing so to not fall, as Lorna came into view, struggling up from the settled dump beneath. She waved him to stay put. His dream-bride was running with sweat, striped primitive with grease and silt. Bleeding from the small wounds of the naked climber. Like him, if young and perfect, she looked like shit.

"How'd it go, here?"

"He's dead," Guy said, with limp indication of the idealogue. "I don't understand a word of Spanish, but I know you couldn't be in two places at once."

"She was on her face," Lorna told him of the other occupant. "I tried to turn her, and saw all the blood. Then, I didn't dare move her. She died pretty fast. I was ogling all the science specimens, stored. Cases galore, glass. A lot's smashed. 'S a smeary mess, shards thrown in."

"That'd be the nose of this thing, from where we're standing, right? The top?"

Lorna nodded, scratching her cheek, which left jagged crimson marks.

"It has a Nazi cross on it," she said, "but why is it shaped like a bell?"

"More like why the-Hell is it here," said Guy.

"There was nothing in the sky, there," said Lorna. "I was staring at that very spot. This thing came out of nowhere, it wasn't there and it was."

"These people are Spanish," Guy wondered out loud.

"Hispanic," she corrected.

"They *spoke* Spanish," he said, testy, seeming angrier for the red rash building at his forehead. "That's a long way from a Munich beer hall."

"All I can tell you is, they carried medical laboratory stuff. A lot, broke open. It's lit down...up there, but I didn't see much past glass."

She ran her hands over her sopping arms and chest, palms smearing her creamy skin dark pink in a trail. Neither took note, as their breathing began heavy. Bellows-strong.

"None of it makes sense," Guy said, frowning down at the dead man, fascinated at the mock of a uniform, the "fruit salad" of medals.

He then repeated the phrase after Lorna repeated it to him, and the young pair, stimulated for indiscernible reasons, kissed as in a movie of old, pawing akin to softcore porn. They marked one another red-stained, even by lips. Their lips were swollen, and comic.

"Thissah delivereeship," he announced, slurring.

"Uhh... Yahh...!" the rejoinder, even lower.

The creatures as mutating, could hear the atmosphere around them. Life at earliest epoch, spoke, in their minds. The name "Peron", already forgotten. Thoughts as received, words as images, were commanding. Hot.

In last crumbs of humanness, the man said, "The Future..."

Lorna hopped, emoting she-beast.

"*We're innit, Guy!*", happy screaming, bellowing from maw three times increased, and a hatch above blew in, armed commando in its wake.

Though overcome, subhumans both reacted with proper shock, as said hatch exploded down, a dozen feet away. Commando bound to springy cable, seated balanced, was Army...rather, an agent dressed for downtime, canteen, kickin' it. Booted, panted camou, armed...stripped to black muscle tank, default style of only one raider, and she of pixels. Diesel black crew cut, eyes of war sweeping all angles. The reddening Guy Teague and Lorna Jensen, were morphed to bestial perception. The intruder, sharp demands in an English become already too complex, gestured with her weapon, something the young monsters better understood. Lorna, crouching, flashed great teeth, saliva faucet-running; Guy, raised trunks of arms, stepping forward.

Dara Jane “Hatchling” Tork, rogue on assignment to certain suicide, was unmasked. Having shed all latex. Protected from every toxin comprising capsule's environment, by only warrior's meds: the rifle in her hands. Widemouth, nothing common, it fired small grenades, delayed internal detonation. Hatchling put two into Guy, then another into Lorna's skull, and on a one-count, drew fetal into her sling.

The sound was akin to a riot in the Produce section. Hatchling, legging out of her saddle, saw dollops had touched boot laces, steel toes. She knew her life was over, no issues there, and agents weren't squeamish. The goo of the contagion, was merely unwelcome. Breathing that unseen, was enough.

Knowing layout, mentally flipping the blueprints, Tork picked her way, champion mountain climber, through wrecked clutter and garbage, to where the seeding DNA was set into the nose. In fact, the revolving-stack cases, 5 figures' worth of specimens, had been locked in, uniform. Less than half sat nominally in place, now.

Politely spitting away from the dead woman beneath her, Hatchling Tork nonetheless planted a rubber sole to small of the corpses' back, surveying. She knew she was already contaminated; this was a one-way mission, but for that, she assessed only the job at hand, never hesitating. Out of attached gear came a mini-Uzi, far upgraded. Packed with bare, uncased ammo which exploded to dots at impact. Swimmer's goggles tied into remaining ducky at nape of her neck, were pulled, stretched and snapped to place. Upward focused, and....

Hatchling emptied the entire load, cyclic setting, going the round of genetic lockers no matter apparent damage. Until the Israeli firearm was spent, blowing smoke, her finger stayed clamped on the trigger. Tucked hard to shoulder. Spray of glass and metal geometrically increased by the fragmenting bullets. There was a tearing sting, another, another...but eyes protected, unerring, ingrained knowledge of The Life as operative, the realization of Death soon to grip her hand...Dara Jane Tork stayed "don't give a shit"-calm. As with the grenade launcher, the mini-Uzi was tossed to deck. Goggles thrown back, to dangle. The rogue climbed again, in reverse.

Toeholds, return climb a jungle gym, entry-level stuff. Tork was fast to her sling, the saddle, strapping in. Regarding red beasts terminated. Literally glowing warm, the bodies a useless uranium. What would exit the Nazi Bell this far secluded, would weaken, mutate to dampened poisons, weak viruses. What remained, if authorities, slow, were worried of selfpreservation, bore presto change-o half life. Likely, there'd be deaths. Brief national news, screaming print. Between 1980's paranoia and limited quantity, History would show it flash, a fire in the night. "A mere bag of shells", a neighbor's words in Dara's childhood. Probably boost paranormal interest. But Hatchling Tork had faith in US Intelligence.

Watching the laundry pile of glowing dead, frowning, she coded in to keypad at her hip. Still armed,

Hatchling knew she could just take off her own head. She didn't want that. The service drone would lift her heavenward, then far out to sea. Many miles, until its taxed batteries would through weakness, lower her to the ocean...and into. What organic poisons killed there, in faceless deep, would be little and nothing, then diluted. Made gone. Some dead fish, oh, yay. She'd always preferred a good burger.

The cables, vinyl with superior give, tightened. The agent stared unmoved at the glow-mess, considering stupidity, and that of humanity. Efficient if not effortless, she was drawn up from the killer confines of the very destroyed Nazi Bell...

...and out, into hot wind of the Pacific, hard, deep blue everywhere. No California beach, no America but by way of old patriotism—Hatchling Tork hung 3/4's out but not free of the empty belly of "concrete battleship" Fort Drum. The miniature Philippine island converted to stationary "ship", ominous fortress warning enemies away. Burnt blackened, long past. Ruins. Above, 'copter blades churned. Hatchling instantly focused above. A helicopter no heavier than standard transport had her, not the service drone. Her mind used precious seconds, absorbing the time slip. Or perhaps she'd been grabbed by a competitor, her act too impulsive for those calculating. No matter her Self had no apparent change, she was captive. The whirlybird's blue and white recognized on a wide bank of the hovering craft, had Tork cursing. Arm back far behind, one handed, immediate grip. The riot shotgun, a Smith and

Atchisson beta, small load micro-rockets, was out, and brought close to pump.

A bullet, soft of her right shoulder, basic stuff...but the blast, disabling, a punch deep in, metallic bee swarm. The shotgun dipped askew, then fell off her lap, useless, into the belly of the hollowed fortress, as another projectile slammed her left shoulder immobile. Tork's head lolled, and the saddle held by vinyl lines, was briefly baby rocker. The rogue fought for control, biting blood from her lower lip.

Further up, toward the contrived "bow" of the old military experiment, a figure peeping elfin, bright, around a dark brown turret. Rostaquer du Mat of The Colonial, once dead, waved a shiny .22 not bigger by one inch than his grip. The imp made his pistol jiggle, sun's glint fooling trick of fast spin. Rostaquer smiled, very satisfied.

"Ah-ah-*AHH...!*" he mocked, high comedy warning. "You're reacting. Not thinking."

Her speech center obeyed, but low names and lurid assessments past her bleeding lips had no power, and du Mat rose, first pretending to listen, cupping an ear, shaking head, then with deft movements, signaling the chopper. The sponge of her saddle now coddling trap, lifted Hatchling Tork out and off Fort Drum. The rust and broken concrete, useless cannon and dry, dead brown, slid away, and she was being taken prisoner.

"You smiling bastard!" she managed. "The world's disease, now! Kill me! *Kill me!*"

"You're going to China," he told her, hearty. Resonant.

"Though, they don't want 'guests' like you. I've a reservation, made--they'll patch your wings, treat you and street you! Look me up, if any 'I' exists, *any*where!"

Hatchling roared, but the anger, the shouting had her sick all over herself, and she could only stare, ruined for the moment, as her inquisitor in gray tweed and deerstalker cap posed dramatic atop browned deck--affecting Bond, poster silhouette. She knew the man, reborn for purposes, thought he knew what he was doing...but none of them had any idea. Her executing the first monsters to then drown herself, had been the better strategy.

A stone wall short, sunk into other Pacific depths, air acrid and thick with smoke of busy ordnance. Revolution-era clad down to tricorns, throwback militia armed with wide bore shotguns double-barreled, the Colonial's "Bluecoat Squad", labored as cast in archival cartoon. Blasting endless at interlopers trespassing more frequently with the months. Trout-sized, the schools of fish determined to make landing. Driven by instinct artificially instilled. An effect and symptom of the Peronist red contagion. Fish overwhelmingly of bone, malevolent. Keying on any destination which denied them. The waters of splintered dead, were thick with dark burgundy. The Bluecoats, fully inoculated, screened weekly, were proud operatives grown hardened. Banter, similes and comparisons to Bunker Hill, even curses, had become boots planted to stone wall low-slung, explosive shells never keeping an

Irresistible Force from returning.

The blasts, constant, battlefield worthy, continued, uneven chorus. The sounds, carried; Torch Island, large enough for the cadre, sported a fine westerly wind, today. As claps and crushing blows in a fight, they carried to the grounds where Taddeo and Woodpecker, near tarpaulin shielding water, moved in kata. The tricky, avoidant kind. Every angle as used for attack, close in, no contact. To touch your opponent even lightly, to graze, was considered a foul; to have to rely on known defense to block, was minus a point. The couple kept track of minuses, in their heads. A perfect session, meant ending 0-0.

Uninhibited, having learned from antiquity, the married warriors sparred naked; their session had continued for some time, and with the added effort of avoiding touch, small breaths, gasps, escaped both. Concentration on agility giving way after long, unabated movement, to concentration on avoiding a negative, which cheapened the exercise. Woodpecker felt a tendon shiver as she planted that foot back, and stepped in retreat, signaling him.

"Done," she said. "Zero."

"Zero," he added, and both gulped air, Taddeo, hands on hips. "God*dam*, your speed...!"

"About three-quarters in, that was all I had," said Woodpecker, beeline for the water chest.

Handoff, and both poured water, drank water, fed one another the same and drenched them. Into embrace, which was too hot, then more H2O and slow stretches.

Their work demanded staying supple, and both agents, veterans of countless missions, sported wounds which, though healed, must never remain static.

Because of their reality and Peronist colonies within it...not counting the mutations zoned off by electric currents and laser, the red contagion infecting so many then made vanished...especially because of their life lived and why, Taddeo and Woodpecker knew themselves as changed, remade. Divergent, not themselves...a foolish consideration, whether or not one believed in string theory. Only the husband, knew with certainty he was new, reliving what had been his life, before, but he could never get used to it, and it troubled Robert Viscom, once a townie kid among others near Cold War Akron. To grasp Life as everywhere constant. Constantly remade.

As his companion. Woodpecker, Taddeo had known from her cradle. She'd been his kid sister's hanger-on friend, the tagalong of that group. Devoted to and under the bootheel of a mad heroin addict of a mother, back when you didn't see such stuff in Pleasantville, USA. There was no crush, but it wouldn't have mattered. Taddeo left for Gabon and the Peace Corps in 1964, as he had originally. Stayed in Africa, mercenary soldier, through the Nigerian Civil War. Unlike "actual history", he had come back to Ohio secretly, in '71, at Christmas. Run into her by chance, sad, empty nursemaid to her dying mom. The waste of potential, made him sick. In a display much out of character, Taddeo evangelized The Colonial, the Life awaiting one who wanted it enough. Serendipity was in play; the suffering mom died the night before Taddeo was to leave. After that, it was transformation time. She so long scared of her own shadow became a scary shadow instead, one made happy by her power, fulfilled via authority and skill. As daring as her husband, less apt to favor mercy.

In the original timeline, often referred to as “The Ultimate Reality”, he and Woodpecker had been strangers: Taddeo, as he was now, but she, a gang chieftess of city streets, anarch, brilliant mind among the low, intent on the bright blaze toward “good-looking corpse”. Taddeo, more than 20 years her senior, had recruited her on the fly, in the middle of a mission. He knew this from hard copy left in rooms of stasis by his original, “Ultimate” self. Leadership permitted no leaping ahead in knowledge. It was only a month ago, he'd “caught up to Them” and been permitted to know.

Disconcerting, offsetting. The splinter, too hard of “real”. All senses told him nothing essential had changed. Foolish, but Taddeo would say he was the same, it was his lifemate and teammate, his fellow operative who differed. His original self, not one for lengthy notes, gave a detailed description of “his” Woodpecker. But for a mole or three, a scar or four, no difference Taddeo could suss. He admitted he didn't know what to do with a 20-year gap, opposed to only several between them, now.

Into cool down. Him, curling into yogic crouch, to pop free stubborn connective tissue; her, performing what others termed "anatomically impossible" stretching. So many twists, turns, bends, short counts, and they were toweling off, grinning.

A hail, thick European. Carmesim, sister agent, was out of quarantine, headed their way. Woodpecker, to whom the woman, German-Portugese, was close friend, cheered with fists upraised.

It had been 30 days since Carmesim and her partner returned. That they'd required twice the normal two-week seclusion for incoming undercovers, spoke to the job at hand: compiling and tracing the 'why' of transformative escalation. The world, still hard in opposition to Peronist takeover, having zoned off all mutant monsters, was lately encountering worse.

"On a day so bright, air so good!", said the tall, blonde woman, hands waving happy in manner of the freed. "All you do is train! Soldiers for real! How dull!"

Woodpecker mimicked the handwaving, jiggling as in a dance. Beaming.

"*Sister,*" she said, taking Carmesim in deep embrace. "So glad you cleared!"

"The extra half week, was because Assegai did not," replied Carmesim, accented in the thick, low German she still possessed. The pair came out of their embrace misty-eyed and fearful, in that order.

"Red...?"

"*Nein, nein*...calm," said Carmesim, nodding the same at Taddeo. "It's...the Peronists have found a way to replicate the red contagion. Revert it, once more to be their own. I delivered all microfilm, but doubt it helps."

"'Technology to advance warmaking'," Taddeo quoted from the propaganda he'd so often heard. "They have no interest in the short route, do they?"

"I hear that," said Carmesim, grim. "'Still going to be a sea of two people. What was their scripture?...'Id't..it's you'..."

"*It's you who are going to change*," said Woodpecker over her shoulder, sideways to them, dressing now. "This is payloads worse than all-bone fish."

Taddeo, anger just below his coldness, asked Carmesim, "Assegai didn't clear? He's infected, to re-become a P..."

"He already has, Tad," she said.

Taddeo began at the holding area, more than a mile away, in a dash.

"*He's already gone, Tad!*"

Slow turn. A sweep of endless sky, as if Creation was traitorous. A godlike enemy. Taddeo faced her again. He had worked with Carmesim for more than ten years, since she had joined.

"I'm clean," she announced, with embedded Teutonic dignity. "But, how long any of us stays so? Let us pitch coins, my brother."

"Bro," said Woodpecker, signaling, at last into clothes, feet hooking into thongs from behind, by hand.

His gaze to hers. A chill, firing to overheat. She used "bro" often to address him, e.g. agents still home town neighbors. His original self had written her pet name in The Ultimate, was "pro". His for her—another, deeper chill—was the same in both realities.

"Peck?"

"Contagion breaks guns," she said, not trying for poetry. "History covers contagion.

"I love you," she continued, "but, the time insertion tests? Almost ready for people. I'm volunteering for The First Century with you or with anyone, or alone."

Well. On your mark, get set... Paratroops over the side.

Taddeo told her, "We'll shower, then report. 'Ready that way immediately, for Medical."

2012. Hours before what would gain arcane notoriety as "The Mandela Effect". Taddeo, Woodpecker, as they had been, with foreknowledge provided through materials delivered via dimension. They stood halfway up a rise of green, back end of the landing strip, near-distant to Dark Jade's ready transport. Rostaquer was with them. This was the mission, solo, when 'it' happened. Woodpecker would avoid mortal illness, here, but du Mat's fateful mission had no choice but to occur. Too much in Time, was mandated. Things followed a course. Only those simple, minus understanding, said, "Just don't go."

There were options, feints and tricks this time, arming the agent. The ambush which had one time erased him, a close-in betrayal, would hurt and suffer loss, unlike that first "take". Rostaquer's reactive talents, were world class. His knowing--when as it unfolded originally, he could not have--would freeze a few. Buy seconds. The chosen assassin's family, would never see his face, again. But, it had been, *was* a steel trap.

Precision, layered. As Jim Bowie of legend, upon his deathbed, the Colonial agent was in wait with back up, and primed—walls were still walls, if of ranks.

They'd said their goodbyes, made their pledges. Reminded of the best which sat well with the others. Here, rechecks, this usage of item, that avenue of escape. Rostaquer, knowing in Time each Taddeo, every Woodpecker was working at this puzzle. One of mosaic scraps. His, was a special feature. Easter egg. Extra credit. Possibly, only the two anywhere cared about the third. Like the dirge went, what a lucky man he was.

The bumblebee of a craft, speedster close to supersonic, fired up, piercing roar. No impatience involved. None had need to check their timepieces.

Always dapper in deerstalker of the Great Holmes, neat as a pin in tweed jacket... older now, as they all were...Rostaquer absorbed the feel of the minute, the acceptance within. Their faces. In Time, what faces and being, what many hearts were there, real? Bonded, caring, giving a shit. Souls, spirits infinitesimal, only one, and who they were.

Taddeo offered his hand. Rostaquer received it, and they lingered in this. Woodpecker, always there to take the piss out of him, reached to grip Rostaquer's shoulder. Might of three the equal of armies, reduced to hope.

"You've meant the world," said Taddeo, eyes dry but clouding in protection.

"And every star," added Woodpecker, punctuating with a cuff to their friend's jaw.

Rostaquer du Mat looked at the two, from face to face. He knew, always had, life held what it held. He didn't expect this to work, favors or none. He was satisfied. He had lived. Paid his nickel. Made his choices.

Gently, he placed a hand behind the neck of both, which they allowed. His words held the usual quip, but they were warm words, said in farewell.

"I was only along for the ride. Quite a wild one. Made the company worth it."

And he swept off, then trotted, then ran to Dark Jade's plane. He didn't look back.

"Can we even solve his part?" Woodpecker asked Taddeo, as the craft began to taxi.

"It's a 7-10 split," said Taddeo, drawing her to his shoulder. "I've seen pins do acrobatics, but...

"It's thanks to backwash, if it happens, Peck. We both said prayers, at least as kids."

She looked off to a place past the sky.

"I remember."

They both lifted hands, knowing Rostaquer did not see them, as the private transport shot with enhanced speed, far deep, East.

www.ingramcontent.com/pod-product-compliance
Ingram Content Group UK Ltd.
Pitfield, Milton Keynes, MK11 3LW, UK
UKHW021915190726
13853UKWH00002B/679